Iowa
State Facts

Nickname:	Hawkeye State/Corn State
Date Entered Union:	December 28, 1846 (the 29th state)
Motto:	Our liberties we prize and our right we will maintain.
Famous Iowa Men:	William F. "Buffalo Bill" Cody, *scout* Johnny Carson, *TV entertainer* Herbert Hoover, *U.S. president* Glenn Miller, *bandleader*
Flower:	Wild prairie rose
Tree:	Oak
Fact:	The town of Fort Atkinson was the site of the only fort ever built by the U.S. government to protect one Indian tribe from another.

The gentle demand of his mouth sent shock waves through her body,

and Julie's resolution to keep the kiss brief and casual vanished. Long moments later, he raised his head and said huskily, "I've been wanting to do that for an hour, since I first saw you."

She was dimly aware that she was making a fool of herself, kissing a perfect stranger. "It must have been terribly difficult to wait so long for your gratification."

He smiled. "Well, if we're talking about gratification, it would take more than just a kiss."

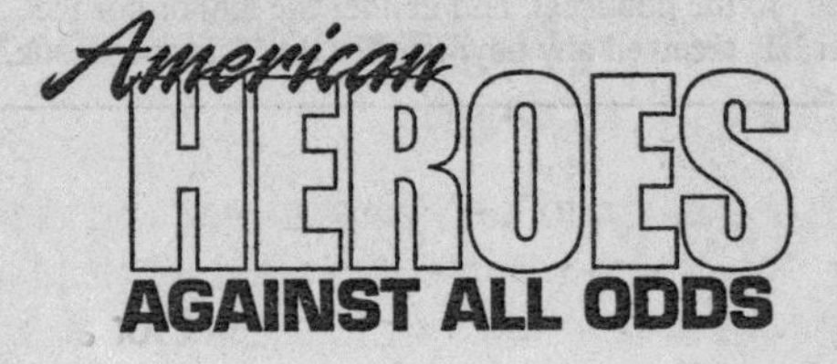

LEIGH MICHAELS

Exclusively Yours

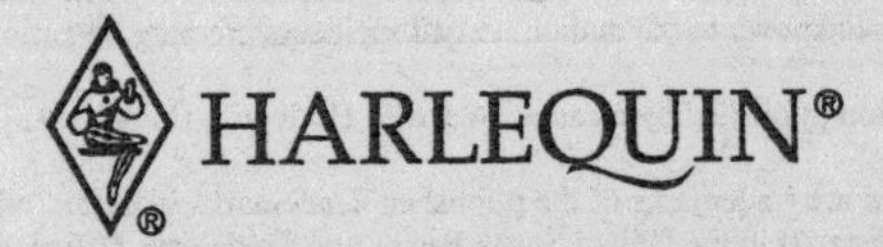

TORONTO • NEW YORK • LONDON
AMSTERDAM • PARIS • SYDNEY • HAMBURG
STOCKHOLM • ATHENS • TOKYO • MILAN • MADRID
PRAGUE • WARSAW • BUDAPEST • AUCKLAND

HARLEQUIN BOOKS
225 Duncan Mill Road, Don Mills,
Ontario, Canada M3B 3K9

ISBN 0-373-82213-8

EXCLUSIVELY YOURS

This edition published by arrangement with Harlequin Books S.A.

Visit us at www.eHarlequin.com

Printed in U.S.A.

About the Author

Leigh Michaels is the author of more than sixty contemporary romance novels for Harlequin Books. She wrote her first romance novel when she was fifteen and burned it, then wrote and burned five more complete manuscripts in the next ten years before submitting to a publisher. A native Iowan, Leigh Michaels welcomes mail from readers. Write to her in care of PBL Limited, P.O. Box 935, Ottumwa, IA 52501-0935.

Books by Leigh Michaels

Harlequin Romance

On September HIll #2657
Wednesday's Child #2734
Come Next Summer #2748
Capture a Shadow #2806
†O'Hara's Legacy #2830
‡Sell Me a Dream #2879
Strictly Business #2951
Just a Normal Marriage #2987
Shades of Yesterday #2997
*No Place Like Home #3010
Let Me Count the Ways #3023
*A Matter of Principal #3070
An Imperfect Love #3086
‡An Uncommon Affair #3119
Promise Me Tomorrow #3141
Temporary Measures #3160
*Garrett's Back in Town #3171
Old School Ties #3184
‡The Best-Made Plans #3214
*The Unexpected Landlord #3233
Safe in My Heart #3248
Ties That Blind #3263
The Lake Effect #3275
*Dating Games #3290
A Singular Honeymoon #3300
Traveling Man #3311
‡Family Secrets #3324
The Only Solution #3337
House of Dreams #3343
Invitation to Love #3352
Taming a Tycoon #3367
†The Unlikely Santa #3388
The Only Man for Maggie #3401
The Daddy Trap #3411
Marrying The Boss! #3423
The Perfect Divorce #3444
Baby, You're Mine! #3463
The Fake Fiancé #3478
• The Billionaire Date #3496
• The Playboy Assignment #3500
• The Husband Project #3504
Her Husband-To-Be #3541
The Boss and the Baby #3552
The Tycoon's Baby #3574

Harlequin Presents

Kiss Yesterday Goodbye #702
Deadline for Love #811
Dreams to Keep #835
**Touch Not My Heart #876
Leaving Home #900
**The Grand Hotel #1004
Brittany's Castle #1028
Carlisle Pride #1049
Rebel With a Cause #1068
†A New Desire #1147
Exclusively Yours #1162
‡Once and For Always #1245
With No Reservations #1266

Harlequin Anthologies

My Valentine 1991
"Some Kind of Hero"

† Tyler-Royale Series
‡ Springhill Series
* McKenna Series
**The Logan Brothers
• Finding Mr. Right!

Dear Reader,

Writing *Exclusively Yours* was like going home. I lived in Des Moines, Iowa, where the story is set, for several years, and I regularly drove down Grand Avenue, past many great old houses, mostly now offices and businesses. One of those houses always caught my eye because of the detailing in its red brick walls and chimneys. It looked lonely—as if it needed someone to love it. So when I wrote about a gift shop called Exclusively Yours, it was a natural choice to put it in that lonely, grand old house.

I hope you'll enjoy the story—and the house—as much as I have!

Leigh Michaels

CHAPTER ONE

'I DON'T think you quite understand, Miss Gordon,' said the cultured, professionally friendly voice of the estate agent. 'I have a client who is interested in buying your house. Would tomorrow be a convenient time for us to look at it?'

Julie Gordon shifted her hold on the telephone receiver, took a firm grip on her manners, and said, politely enough, 'And I don't think *you* quite understand *me*. My house is not for sale.'

The agent laughed a little. 'In my experience, everything is for sale at the right price, and my client is quite willing to pay the price.'

'I'm afraid I'll have to be an exception to your rule.'

'I don't think you'll be disappointed by the arrangements, and I believe this is your best chance at a sale. Your land is quite valuable, but it's small, and buyers for that sort of property aren't easy to find, you know.'

'Good,' Julie said. 'Because I'm not interested in selling, and I'm too busy to have the pleasure of talking to you any more, so will you please not bother me again.' She put the telephone down with a bang. 'What do I have to do to convince these people that I'm not going to sell my house?' she muttered.

The blonde woman across the room looked up from the cash register, where she was counting out the day's receipts. 'I thought you told him last time he called to go drown himself in the Raccoon River.'

'I did. I don't think he believed me. They just don't take no for an answer, Sara.'

The young woman looked troubled. 'Perhaps you should consider it, Julie. It wouldn't hurt to talk to him. After all, it *is* a big house, and it costs a fortune to keep it up—'

'It's my money,' Julie said stubbornly. 'I earn it, and if I want to put a new roof on this house instead of taking a trip to Europe, that's my business.'

'Have you forgotten that your aunt might have something to say about it? She does still own half of it.'

'Aunt Randie loves this house just as much as I do.'

'Oh?' Sara asked drily. 'Does that explain why she takes every opportunity to leave?'

'She's visiting friends in Omaha, Sara.'

'She's always visiting friends. She's been gone for two weeks now.'

'She has lots of friends.'

Sara made a noise that might have been disapproval. 'I think you should at least ask Randie what she thinks about it.'

'She'll be home in a couple of days. I'll tell her about it, but Randie doesn't want to sell the house any more than I do.'

Sara sighed. 'Did you even ask how much the offer was?'

'Sara, you're money-mad.'

'And *you* are a dreamer. Honey, there are other people in the world who adore old houses as much as you do.'

'Those people didn't grow up here. So this house can't possibly mean as much to them as it does to me.'

'What about Randie? You can't make me believe she wouldn't be interested in the money. She's on a pension, and if these people can afford to pay your price, they can also afford to keep the place up a whole lot better than the two of you can.'

'Or they could turn around and sell it to the highest bidder.'

'That is a problem,' Sara conceded. 'But if they really like the house, they wouldn't do that.'

'People who want gorgeous houses to live in are not looking for them in this neighbourhood,' Julie pointed out. 'Whoever wants to buy this house has ulterior motives, you can count on that. The estate agent pointed out himself that the land is what's really valuable. And I won't sell my house so someone can tear it down and replace it with an abomination like that office tower they're building up the street.'

Sara sighed. 'I suppose you're right. But really, Julie, aren't you being just a little stiff-necked about this whole thing? With a good price for this house, you could buy a little shop somewhere, rent an apartment, and have money left over—'

'If Aunt Rosa had intended for this to be a commercial development, she could have sold the house any time in the last fifteen years. She didn't—she left it to Randie and me. And we have no intention of selling it.' Julie turned the key in the heavy brass lock on the front door, closing her little shop for another day. 'I'm going to take Leicester for a walk.' The ancient basset hound snoozing at her feet woke with a jerk at the sound of his name.

'Don't be long,' Sara warned. 'We can't be late to Lynne's wedding.'

'I think I might just skip it, Sara. It's not as if Lynne is really a friend, or anything.' Besides, she told herself, I hate weddings. But she'd really rather not try to explain that to Sara.

'She's been one of your best customers.'

'That's not the same thing. And I won't know anybody there.'

'You could loosen up and meet somebody new.'

'Sara, don't start matchmaking again.'

'Somebody's got to. You don't seem to be interested.'

'I have a perfectly adequate love-life,' Julie said stiffly.

'Is adequate all you want? You haven't had more than three dates with any one man since I've known you. What's the matter with you, Julie? Your someone special isn't just going to walk into the shop some day—you're going to have to look for him.' She sighed. 'I just don't understand you.'

'Then it's fortunate,' Julie said sweetly, 'that I'm paying you to be my sales assistant, and not my psychologist.' She snapped a leash on to the basset hound's collar and took him out of the side door and down the driveway. Almost immediately, she regretted what she had said; Sara was a good friend, as well as an employee, and she had the best of intentions. It was just that, as a happily married woman herself, she thought that matrimony was the only natural state for the human female.

I'll apologise as soon as I get back, Julie told herself. And I'll go to the wedding like a good girl, and I'll pretend to enjoy myself.

Julie didn't begrudge Sara her husband; but not every woman could be as fortunate in her choice of men as Sara, and Julie had decided long ago that living alone was far better than chancing another disaster. No, she didn't covet Sara's marriage. It was her little daughter that Julie envied. Kristen was a blue-eyed angel who could make Julie's heart melt.

I could have had a Kristen of my own, she thought, and bit her lip hard. What point was there in thinking of that tonight? Those days with Keith were long past. It was over, and she no longer wept into her pillow over the unfairness of it all. Except, now and then, when she had this desperate longing for a child that was flesh of her flesh, blood of her blood...

Enough, she told herself. She would, as she had for the last five years, find her solace in the children of friends. That, and her business, and her house, would keep her busy. It was enough for a good life, she thought. It would have to be.

She picked her way across the ruts in the makeshift driveway of the construction site, where the office tower was rising slowly skywards. Mud carried by the heavy trucks had spread in irregular trails and then baked hard under the relentless heat of the mid-western sun, until now it was a hazard to every pedestrian. She looked up with disfavour at the steel skeleton which was rising beam by beam. How much higher would the building go? she wondered. They were up ten floors now and, on the highest level, men in hard hats walked about on the narrow beams as casually as if they were in their own living-rooms.

At her feet, the basset hound whined. Julie looked down at the mournful animal. 'Are you impatient to get on with your walk, Leicester?' she asked. 'You don't see anything beautiful about that abominable building either, do you? And all that noise must hurt your ears.'

She looked with irritation at the large red and blue letters on the hoarding at the front of the property, which announced that this was the site of a new generation of energy-efficient office tower construction.

'Who cares if it's more efficient?' she muttered to herself. 'They're destroying history to put up concrete boxes, and in thirty years they'll be tearing them down to try out another innovation. And in the meantime, buildings that would have lasted hundreds of years are gone for ever.' She closed her eyes with a tiny twinge of pain, remembering the buildings that had been here—buildings that had been put up when Des Moines was a raw new town and Grand Avenue was no more than a country road.

'It's a sin,' she told Leicester as they turned towards home. 'The people who are doing this should be shot. Or locked up in their miserable buildings, and fed bread and water once a day. That's what these places look like—prisons!'

And now, she thought, they want to do this to my house, too—tear it down, and put up another glossy, anonymous tower in its place.

She looked up at her house with a critical frown. The three-storey red-brick structure was of no particular architectural style. The pillared front porch was a fragment of Greek revival; the white stone trim that arched above the leaded glass windows suggested Federal influence. The wrought-iron railing along the upstairs balcony hinted at a Mediterranean origin. The building wasn't fanciful or elegant; it was just a solid old house, unpretentious and rugged, like the tough-minded Iowa pioneers who had built it.

Here and there, the house showed its age. The intricate brickwork in the chimney needed tuck-pointing. The front porch could use a coat of paint. And some time this summer she was going to have to find a very tall ladder and spend a couple of days puttying windows. Sara was right; the bills were horrible. But Julie didn't care. This was home.

Leicester tugged on the leash. 'All right,' Julie said. 'I know I shouldn't be dawdling—I should be getting dressed this very minute, or I'll miss Kristen's grand appearance as the flower girl.' That was what she would do, she decided. She would concentrate on Kristen tonight, and perhaps the wedding itself wouldn't bother her.

She took a short cut across the concrete car park that belonged to the insurance agency next door. The area was empty now, with business hours over. It was aggravating, she thought, that they'd been able to pave that space to within a few feet of her side door. But the entire area was zoned for commercial development now, and that meant that a property owner could do nearly anything he liked with every inch of his land.

A hundred years ago, she thought, as she stared across the broad avenue, this whole neighbourhood had been the choice of the city's élite. Then it had been lined with houses, big, elegant homes where families had been raised and mourned, where business transactions had been planned, where the affairs of states had been negotiated. Now, it was just another commercial block. And, she had to admit, even she had joined that parade. Her eyes rested on the discreet sign near the kerb in front of her house. 'Exclusively Yours', it said, in flowing script.

That's different, she told herself robustly. She hadn't destroyed the house, or cut it up. She was merely running an antiques and gifts shop in it, catering to a very élite clientele. After all, something had to be done to pay the bills. Economics—that was why so many of the houses along Grand Avenue were gone now, sacrificed on the altar of progress.

Julie straightened her shoulders with determination. My house, she told herself flatly, will not be one of the ones that disappear. If I have to say no to that estate agent for a hundred years—or drown him in the Raccoon River myself—I will not give up my house, and let it be destroyed.

The Botanical Centre was a small geodesic dome nestled on the bank of one of Des Moines' two rivers. It was flooded with lights when they walked up the long stretch of pavement and past the brightly coloured stainless-steel sculpture that doubled, when no adults were looking, as a climbing gym for the younger set.

'Trust Lynne to have an unusual wedding,' Julie said. 'Antique lace in a glass dome.'

'I'd have expected her to choose one of the really gorgeous churches— Kristen, you may not walk through the sculpture, because your hoopskirt won't fit.'

Kristen looked stubborn for a minute, as if she'd like to try it out to be sure her mother was telling the truth, but she sighed and smoothed her white lace skirt and walked along like a lady instead.

'Well, she certainly didn't do it because she couldn't afford to decorate a church with flowers.' Julie pulled open the heavy door.

Sara laughed. 'I'd like to try living on Lynne Hastings' budget for a while,' she agreed. 'It would be nice to find out how the daughter of an insurance company president manages to make ends meet.'

'She owns part of that company, you know; her father put it in trust for her when she was born.'

'Did she tell you that?'

'Of course not. It was in the newspaper last week. They had a story about the insurance company going public.'

'I wish I'd had that kind of luck.' Sara took Kristen off to the side room, where the wedding party was getting ready.

Julie wandered along the paths under the high glass dome, looking at the exotic plants without really seeing them, while she waited for the guests to gather.

Would there ever again be a wedding she could enjoy? she wondered. Would there be a time when white lace and orange blossom and two china figures atop a cake brought sentimental tears instead of angry memories?

It isn't Lynne's fault that Keith dumped you, Julie lectured herself. You should be happy for her because she's marrying the man she loves, and not jealous because five years ago the man you loved married another girl.

It isn't fair, she thought. If I'd been Lynne, and my father owned an insurance company, he'd have married me...

She caught herself up short. You wouldn't have wanted him that way, she told herself. Not if you had to buy him.

The bride was beautiful in her antique lace; unhampered by the restrictions of a budget, her dressmaker had produced a wedding gown that would probably set a new standard on the society pages.

It was a gorgeous ceremony. The lovely words of the old service were accompanied by the muted splashing of the waterfall that fed the goldfish pool. The glass dome was an ideal amphitheatre for the string orchestra. Kristen was the perfect five-year-old angel as she walked through the aisle of guests and scattered rose-petals on the path. And the adoration in Lynne's eyes as she gazed up at her new husband was so painfully beautiful that Julie had to look away.

She was standing on one of the staircases that led up to the balcony. As she turned her head, so she didn't have to look at the two young people making their vows on the pathway below, her eyes fell on a man on the lower level, and for a moment her lungs refused to function. It can't be him, she thought. It's only a physical resemblance, someone who looks a little like him. I haven't seen him in years; I might not even know him. And why would he be here?

But of course he would be at Lynne's wedding, she realised. Keith Evans could be seen these days at any event where the powerful and wealthy of Des Moines' society could be found. Keith would not dare to miss an event where so many of his potential clients would be gathered.

I'm the one who is out of place here, Julie thought wryly. Keith is perfectly at home with these people. And his wife—her family must be related to Lynne's. These people all seem to be cousins of one sort or another. How could I have forgotten that?

He hasn't seen me, she thought. As soon as the ceremony is over, I'll find Sara and tell her I want to go home. I'll tell her I have a splitting headache—

Then her spine straightened with pride. Why should she run away? Why should she have to explain anything? So what if she came face to face with Keith Evans? He was the one who should be ashamed of himself—Julie Gordon had nothing to hide.

Julie inspected him, under her lashes. He was beginning to display a paunch, she decided, and his hair—yes, it was thinning in the centre. You'd better get yourself to a health club and a hair-transplant man, Keith, she chided silently. That rich wife of yours can afford it...

She was relieved to find that the shattering pain was gone. She was still angry with herself for being taken in by him—for being weak enough to trust him and to believe for so long in his excuses. But he no longer had the power to hurt her.

It's impossible to be in love with someone who isn't what you thought he was, she decided, and obediently bent her head in prayer with the rest of the guests. You loved the idealised Keith, the honest and upright man you had made up in your head. Then the idol collapsed, and you saw what he was really like...

She was being watched. The sudden sensation was like a prickly insect crawling across her skin with agonising slowness. Her first thought was that Keith had spotted her, but, when she darted a glance in his direction, she saw that he was intently watching the young couple. Slowly, trying to look casual, she let her glance sweep across the assembled guests.

Everyone seemed to be concentrating on the bride and groom as they exchanged rings. It's your imagination, Julie, she told herself tartly. You feel so uncomfortably out of place here that you've imagined that someone is watching you, maybe even laughing at you.

She turned her attention back to the wedding party, and the prickling sensation intensified. She let her eyes sweep across the ushers, who stood with military precision on the pathway. One of them was looking at her...

To the casual observer, there was nothing in his pose to suggest that he wasn't paying attention to what was going on at the altar. But his eyes were intent on Julie, studying her with meticulous care. And he wasn't laughing.

Is my make-up on straight? she wondered with sudden panic. His eyes wandered slowly from her black hair, parted in the centre and pulled back into a madonna-like coil at the nape of her neck, to the icy pink of her dress, to the darker bands of colour at the hemline. I wonder, she thought, if he can tell how badly my knees are knocking right now.

He reached her toes and started up again, pausing along the way to assess her figure, and fury shook Julie to the core. He was obviously stripping her clothes off in his mind; she was just a little entertainment to get him through a boring ceremony. Why not treat him to a little of his own medicine?

She tried. She noted that his dark brown hair was inclined to curl, that his face was deeply tanned against the white of his bow-tie and wing collar, that the black tail-coat was perfectly tailored to broad shoulders and narrow waist. He looked like an athlete, she thought. There was strength in those shoulders, as if he'd done a great deal of manual work. She found herself wanting to look at his hands, and she was disappointed because, like the other ushers, he was wearing white gloves. She found herself wishing that he'd pull them off.

That's foolish, she told herself. From this distance, she couldn't possibly see whether his hands were strong and callused. She tried to imagine him without his clothes, and was startled to realise how easy it was to visualise him that way—

Colour splashed into her cheeks, and she looked away as quickly as she could. She wasn't fast enough, though, to avoid seeing the tiny smile that crossed his mouth. It was a knowing smile, as if he had read her mind.

Conceited snob, she thought. He probably thinks any woman who sees him instantly thinks about what he'd be like in bed.

Which, she reminded herself roundly, was precisely what she'd been wondering. Not that she had any intention of finding out, but a woman could look, couldn't she? Wasn't that what liberation was all about? It didn't mean she was interested in anything more.

She passed through the reception line quickly, and only after noting that the ushers were not part of the formality, then went out to the courtyard for a breath of fresh air. After the heavily humid atmosphere of the tropical garden, the cool breeze against her flushed face was soothing.

She sat down on a bench and watched the trickling fountain, glad that no one had seen her come outside. After the crush of people, it was pleasant to be alone for a moment. She'd go back in a few minutes and be the perfect wedding guest, but for right now she needed the peaceful breeze and the gentle splash of the fountain. Only the muted hum of traffic on the motorway nearby reminded her that she was not alone in the world.

'Eve in the Garden of Eden,' said a husky voice behind her, and Julie jumped.

'Keith!' It was a startled whisper.

'So it really is you.' He sat down on the other end of the bench, careful to leave a genteel distance between them. 'I wondered if I was seeing things. You know, I've never stopped thinking about you—'

'Likewise,' she said coolly, without looking at him. 'I think about you every day.'

He slid closer. 'Oh, Julie, I knew that you couldn't mean it, when you said you never wanted to see me again—'

She interrupted once more. 'I think about how you promised to marry me, just as soon as you were finished with law school and you could afford a wife. I think about how hard I worked to help pay your way, and how I used to plan our wedding and dream about how wonderful our life would be. And I will never forget, Keith, that you didn't even have the guts to tell me yourself that you were marrying another girl. No, you let me read it in the newspaper...' Her voice broke.

Keith's arm was around her shoulders. 'I couldn't bear to see you unhappy, Julie,' he said. 'I know it was cowardly not to tell you, but surely you understand that I was doing it for us—'

Her eyes were as hard as emeralds, and fire flashed in their depths. 'You expect me to believe that you married another girl for my benefit?'

'Of course I did it for you. Stop and think, Julie. It was a short cut—'

'I was perfectly willing to take the long way. You weren't.' Her voice was bitter. She shrugged his arm off her shoulders.

He smiled wryly, as if to say that she didn't understand, and clasped his hands on his knee. 'So tell me about yourself, Julie,' he invited. 'It must be three years since I've seen you.'

'Don't you keep track of your wedding anniversaries?' she asked bitterly. 'It will be five years next month since you married Anita.'

'Really? That long? How time does fly! Are you married?'

'No.'

'Engaged?'

'No.'

He smiled, as if satisfied. 'What are you doing these days?'

'Is it any of your business?'

'I still love you, Julie,' he said huskily. 'That makes it my business.'

'That,' said a voice behind them, 'is your tough luck, Keith. Here's your champagne, darling.'

Before she could even look up, Julie found the cold stem of a tulip glass in her hand. The handsome usher smiled down into her eyes and then sat down beside her. There was little space on the end of the bench, but when she would have moved closer to Keith to make room for the newcomer, she found that the usher's arm had slipped about her waist and was holding her prisoner, clamped against his side. 'Sorry I didn't bring you a glass, Keith,' he added, 'but I had no idea you'd be tasteless enough to barge in on a private party.'

His brown eyes twinkled as he looked down at Julie. There were fine lines around them, as if he spent a lot of time in the sun without dark glasses. And there was a deep cleft in the centre of his chin. Julie found herself wanting to reach up and stroke it.

'I was talking to Julie,' Keith said stiffly.

'I know. And if you'd like to have lunch together some day and catch up on old times, that's fine with me. But tonight is mine, so please go away. Besides, Anita is looking for you, and I don't think she'd like it if she found you out here.'

'Oh.' Keith started towards the door and looked uncertainly back at the pair on the bench. 'I had no idea that you two—'

'I know,' the usher said cheerfully. 'Let's keep it a private story, shall we?' He sipped his champagne and reached across Julie to set his glass down on the bench. Then he took the untasted glass from her numb fingers and said, under his breath, 'Just to convince him, in case he looks back—' His hand tightened against her shoulderblade, pressing her against his chest. Out of the corner of her eye, she could see that Keith had paused in the doorway. She stifled the protest that came automatically to her lips, and let the usher draw her closer still. Just a momentary caress, she was thinking, just to make Keith believe that she had no interest left in him… It was rather nice of this unknown man to step in and protect her.

The gentle demand of his mouth sent shock-waves through her body, and her resolution to keep the kiss brief and casual vanished. The tip of his tongue teased against her teeth. He tasted like champagne. A woman could get drunk just kissing him, she thought, half-consciously.

Long moments later, he raised his head and said

huskily, 'I've been wanting to do that for an hour, since I saw you on the stairs.'

She looked over her shoulder. Keith was gone. She was dimly aware that she was making a fool of herself, sitting here beside the fountain kissing a total stranger. 'It must have been terribly difficult for you to wait so long for your gratification,' she said tartly. Her breath was coming unsteadily.

He smiled. 'Well, if we're discussing gratification, it would take more than just a kiss.'

Julie realised abruptly that she was still in his arms, and that his fingertips were drawing tiny, sensual circles on her shoulderblades. She pulled primly away from him. So much for her picture of him as a knight in shining armour, riding up to save her! He'd been looking out strictly for himself. 'I don't know why you did this—'

'Because I wanted to,' he said promptly. 'And because you looked as if you needed to be rescued. If you'd like to say thank you, I can suggest a very nice way.'

Julie pressed on. 'I can't imagine why you thought it was any of your business. And I did not need to be rescued.'

His eyes narrowed. 'My mistake,' he said coldly. 'I had the impression, you see, that you hadn't seen Keith for a while, and that you didn't want to renew the acquaintance. Is this a game you and Keith play often at parties? No wonder he looked so confused when I popped in.' He picked up his champagne glass and looked at her over the rim as he drank. Then he said, with a soft note in his voice that had nothing to do with gentleness, 'Perhaps you don't know Anita Evans?'

'I know her quite well enough.'

'I suppose Keith has told you that he's a misunderstood husband. That's not true, you know. Anita understands him very well indeed—that's why she's a jealous cat. You'll be far safer with me tonight.'

Julie's eyes opened wide in shock. 'There was nothing going on here!'

'Spare me the innocent blushes, my dear. In another two minutes, Keith would have been kissing you.'

'He would not have been! I wouldn't have allowed it.'

'Let's not argue about that. We would never agree.'

'I don't kiss married men!'

He smiled, a little. 'And what's your system for finding out if they're married?' he asked smoothly. 'I don't recall you asking me if I have a wife. In any case, Anita would have seen plenty, and the resulting scene would have been very messy.' He drained his champagne glass. 'And just in case you want to know why I'm so sure she would have walked in on your passionate interlude—it's because I sidetracked her on my way back here with the champagne.'

'Oh!' The vision of what a scene that would have caused danced through Julie's head.

'Or did you expect her to come running back here, and I messed up your plans?' he speculated. 'Just as well that I did, if that's what happened. Anita won't give up Keith easily—he's cost her far too much, you see.'

'I thought you were protecting Keith.'

'Oh, no. I really don't care what happens to Keith. But Anita is my cousin, and families have to stick together.'

So he was another cousin. Or was he Lynne's brother, perhaps? Apart from the brown eyes, she could see no family resemblance. Oh, what does it matter? she asked herself crossly. 'So you don't want Anita to get the idea that Keith has a friend on the side.'

'Another one,' he corrected. 'I hope you're not egotistical enough to think you're the only one.'

'I don't think anything when it comes to Keith! I didn't plan this, you know. I didn't expect him to be here, and when I saw him, I had no intention of talking to him at all.'

'If you wanted to avoid him,' the usher observed lazily, 'you certainly picked an unusual place. Coming out into the courtyard alone was an open invitation to any man who was interested, you know. I'm amazed that we haven't had a parade.'

The breeze was suddenly chilly against her flushed skin, but the shiver that shook her had nothing to do with the cold. 'Would you just go away?' she whispered.

'When Lynne asked me to be an usher at her wedding, she said that my only duties would be to walk a blushing bridesmaid down the aisle and to make sure her guests enjoyed themselves.'

'Well, you can help me enjoy the wedding by taking yourself back inside and out of my way. I haven't any interest in you.'

'I know,' he said softly. 'Don't you think that's part

of the charm of the situation? Anita will be very careful of Keith for the rest of the evening, so you may as well find other entertainment. As for me, if you don't come back in with me, Lynne will find all sorts of lonely women for me to entertain. Your instinct was right, you know. I don't have a wife to protect me.'

He stroked the dark wings of hair at her temples. She wanted to pull away from him, but she couldn't find the strength to move. His fingers were long and strong, she noted, toughened with hard work, and yet well manicured. 'One magical evening,' he said. 'Who knows where we might end up?'

Her whole body drew up into a tight coil. 'I don't know what you think I am,' she said sharply, 'but I assure you I am not the kind of woman who goes to bed with a man on less than an hour's acquaintance.'

'I wasn't necessarily talking about taking you to bed,' he mused, 'but if you insist—'

She tried to swallow her embarrassment. 'I don't even know your name.' What she had intended to be a haughty proclamation instead sounded just a little wistful.

He smiled a little, as if there was a joke in what she had said. 'I don't know yours, either. Just—Julie.' There was a second's pause, and then he said, quietly, 'Does it really matter?'

She drew herself up tightly and walked away from him, her spine stiff under the narrow straps of her backless dress. What difference does it make what he thinks of me? she asked herself furiously. If he called me a chair, it wouldn't make me one. So why should it bother me that he believes I'm Keith's mistress? It doesn't make it true.

'I'm puzzled,' he said. 'What do you women see in Keith Evans, anyway?'

The women he knew, she thought, probably wouldn't see anything in Keith. Keith was a washed-out watercolour sketch, while this man was an arrogant portrait in brilliant oils... She drew her errant thoughts back from a dangerous path.

'Foolish me,' he mused. He was very much at ease, his long legs stretched across the paving block path. 'I thought, when you looked me over during the ceremony and then came out here, that you were issuing an invitation. I'd really like to know, Julie. What makes Keith so special that you're willing to brave Anita's wrath?'

It was infuriating, to be talked to in such a way. He's an ignorant idiot, she thought, and I'll never see him again. Why waste my breath trying to convince him of anything?

She turned away and watched the water cascade down the smooth stone of the fountain. 'Power,' she said over her shoulder, her words clipped. 'Money. Influence. Does that satisfy your curiosity?'

He came across to her so quietly that she did not hear him. She didn't know that he was behind her until she felt the brush of his starched shirt against her spine, and his hand warm on her shoulder. He bent his head and kissed the nape of her neck. 'In that case,' he said smoothly, 'you'll be much better off with me. Shall we go and dance, my dear?'

CHAPTER TWO

JULIE jerked away from his possessive hand. 'I don't know how to make it any clearer to you,' she snapped, 'but I am not interested in your less than flattering proposals, Mr—'

'Roberts,' he supplied smoothly. 'Gregory Roberts. My friends call me Greg.'

'Oh.' She stared up at him, wide-eyed. I should have recognised him, she thought, but it wasn't a very good picture of him in the newspaper last week.

It had been an old photograph, that was certain, and not a clear one. That was why she hadn't realised which of Lynne Hastings' cousins this handsome and impudent man was. The fact that he was related to the wealthy and powerful Hastings clan wasn't what had sent her pulse-rate into orbit. But Greg Roberts was also the president of Roberts Development Corporation, and that was the company which was building the monstrosity on Grand Avenue—the one that nearly gave Julie ulcers each time she walked by it.

She had to swallow the desire to tell him what she thought of him and his company. There's no point in giving him your opinion of his new office building, she told herself. He'd only get a good laugh out of it.

'I see it makes a difference, now that you know my name,' he said smoothly. 'Well, I don't mind. Shall we rejoin Lynne's party, or go somewhere to start our own?'

She was furious at the implication that she would fall into bed with him, now that she knew he had money and position. Angry colour stained her cheeks. 'Of course it makes a difference,' she snapped, determined to puncture that ballooning ego. 'But not the kind you think. I know enough about you from my own experience, you see, to know that I could never be interested in someone like you. Goodnight.'

'Oh, but it did make a difference,' he said gently. 'If you had seen your eyes get big—'

'Shock,' she said. 'Until then, I thought—' She bit her tongue and began to edge towards the door. What had she been ready to say? *Until I knew your name, I was attracted to you…* Foolish, she told herself. It hadn't been like that at all. Yes, she had to admit that his kiss had been somewhat enjoyable—

And that, she told herself with incorrigible honesty, was the understatement of the year. But the kiss had occurred before the knight had displayed the tarnish underneath his shining armour.

'Well, I guess it doesn't matter to me if you want to play hard to get,' Greg mused. He raised his voice as she reached the door. 'If you're going to walk out on me, don't forget your champagne.'

Julie turned and told him succinctly just what he could do with the forgotten glass of champagne. He looked properly subdued as she left him alone in the courtyard, but there was a gleam in his clear brown eyes that warned her she hadn't heard the last of him yet.

She plunged back into the dome with relief, happy to find herself surrounded by people again. That courtyard had been just a little too lonely for comfort, she told herself, in spite of the fact that Greg Roberts' ego was easily big enough to fill it. She paused beside the sprawling grey-green leaves of a century plant and looked around the dome. She thought she caught a glimpse of Sara's pale blue dress far down the path, but, by the time she made her way across the dome, the woman was gone.

I hate to walk into the reception hall alone, she thought. Everyone else has already gone in, and they'll all be looking at me, wondering who I am.

Don't be an idiot, she scolded herself sternly. It's not like you to have an inferiority complex about a simple thing like walking into a room alone. But with Keith there, and Anita...

At least be honest, she told herself. It would be unpleasant enough to run into them. But it wasn't Keith and Anita who were making her uncomfortable. It was that half-threat, half-promise in Greg Roberts' eyes...

And he's still out in the courtyard, licking his wounds, she reminded herself. If you hurry, you'll be safe. Without an additional second's hesitation, she hurried across to the reception hall.

Most of the guests were already seated for the formal dinner. Julie spotted Sara and went across to her. 'I would have saved you a seat,' Sara said with a shrug, 'but Lynne apparently didn't want her guests huddled into cliques, so she assigned tables. I think you're somewhere towards the front.'

'Couldn't you have swapped place cards?' Julie muttered.

'And get myself in trouble with the Hastings clan? Not likely! Go mingle, Julie. You might meet someone priceless.'

'Sorry to disappoint you, ma'am,' said a voice at Julie's elbow, 'but I'm not going to give her the chance to meet anyone at all—only me.'

Julie saw Sara's eyes widen, and she fought off an attack of hysterical giggles. 'Funny thing, coincidence,' Greg murmured in Julie's ear as he led her across the room. 'Lynne put us at the same table.'

'When?' Julie asked tartly. 'Just now, after you told her to?'

'You are so suspicious, my dear. Perhaps she knows Keith's weaknesses, too. They're not exactly a well-kept secret in this family.'

Well, that had put her precisely in her place. Julie bit her lip. 'If she was so concerned about my behaviour,' she muttered, 'I'm amazed that Lynne invited me at all.'

His eyes were bright, the liquid-brown flaring like a torch. His hand tightened on her elbow, a potent reminder of the way he had held her in the courtyard. 'Oh, I'm not,' he said softly. 'You improve the surroundings.'

That does it, she thought. I am not going to stand here and be pawed by a playboy who acts like an overgrown adolescent. 'If you'll just let go of me,' she said, 'I'd like to go home.'

'Oh, the old "I'm not feeling well" ploy? It would cause something of a scene if you were to walk out now, you know. Come and sit down; I'm sure some food will restore your spirits. I'll promise to be good, if that will relieve your headache.'

It would cause a scene if she left, that was undeniable; the table he was leading her to was next to the bridal couple. Besides, Julie was less than certain that she could break away from him; his hand rested on her elbow with ease, but there was the promise of strength in his fingers.

He felt her reluctance. 'I won't hesitate to stop you if you try to run,' he murmured. 'It should be interesting to see what Keith thinks of your behaviour then.'

She gritted her teeth. 'Shouldn't you be paying court to one of the bridesmaids instead of hanging around me?' she asked.

He pulled Julie's chair out with a flourish. 'You can't get rid of me that easily. Have a strawberry.' He popped a luscious whole berry into her mouth.

Julie thought about spitting it out into his hand, but he was holding the hull between his fingers, waiting for her to bite through the berry, and his thumb rubbed casually across her lips in the intimate caress of a lover. Anyone who was watching, she thought bitterly, would have no trouble in diagnosing that gesture. And, in this crowd, there must be plenty of people watching.

She swallowed the berry and said, huskily, 'I can feed myself, thanks.'

He smiled. 'I know, but as long as I keep your mouth full, I don't have to worry about you biting *me*.'

She turned her back on him, and began a determinedly bright chat with the man to her right. I'll just ignore him, she thought.

But Greg draped an arm over the back of her chair, leaned over her shoulder and joined the conversation.

At the first opportunity, she hissed, 'Why are you doing this? I don't want you, and I certainly don't need your attention!'

He let his gaze drift across the room to where Keith and Anita were sitting stiffly side by side.

Her eyes dropped to the plate before her. She knew what he was thinking. He had so easily concluded that she was the kind of woman who would think nothing of coming between husband and wife. He doesn't even know me, but he's judged me, she thought, and was surprised that the idea was like a needle stabbing deep into her mind.

What difference does it make? she asked herself. After tonight, I'll never see Greg Roberts again. If he wants to entertain himself tonight with the idea that he's protecting his cousin Anita's peace of mind, what effect can it possibly have on me?

She scarcely tasted her food. Later, on the dance-floor, she told herself that she was only staying because she didn't have her own car, and if she sought Sara out, and told her she wanted to go home, there would be no end of questions. Better to endure the evening than to make a fuss, she decided.

Greg was a good dancer, though, she thought, when a slow number brought them close. Under other circumstances, she decided, she might even have enjoyed herself...

Sara caught her at the edge of the dance-floor, late

in the evening. 'I'm taking Kristen home,' she said. 'She's asleep on the path under a banana tree, and I think it's time to get her to bed.'

'I'll be right there,' Julie said, with a breath of relief. She had thought Sara would never be ready to leave!

'Oh, don't rush,' Sara said. 'You're obviously having a good time, and I'm sure Mr Roberts will make sure you get home.' She gave Greg a brilliant smile and was gone before Julie could protest.

'My friend is a little thoughtless,' she said finally. 'She tends to see romance anywhere she looks. You needn't feel obliged to take on the escort duty.'

He grinned. 'I *will* take you home, you know,' he said. 'I just make no promises about when you'll get there. We might find something more entertaining to do.'

'Thanks, anyway, but I'd prefer to take a cab.'

'What a spoilsport you are, Julie. One would think you don't trust me. Besides, the bride and groom are ready to leave; surely you don't want to miss that?' He drew her into the dome.

Lynne was a whirlwind in antique lace as she came across to them. 'I haven't had a chance to say a word to you, Julie,' she said. 'Greg's kept you very busy.'

Try as she might, Julie couldn't see a hidden meaning in that. Lynne was innocence itself.

'You really can't blame me, can you, Lynne?' Greg asked lazily. 'Where have you been hiding this girl, anyway? Why haven't I seen her around before?'

Lynne giggled. 'I found her in a little shop on Grand Avenue called Exclusively Yours. I recommend it to you, Greg. I think you'd find several things there that would impress you.' She winked at Julie. A moment later, the newly-weds were gone.

Julie took a deep breath and turned to look up at Greg. 'Now that Lynne is gone, and your task of keeping me from wrecking her reception has been fulfilled, and the party is breaking up, I intend to go home. Are you planning to stand in my way, or do I have your permission to go call a cab?' There was a cynical twist to her words.

For a moment, he didn't seem to hear her. He was still watching the limousine in the car park, where Lynne's dress formed a blur of white under the strong lights. Keith and Anita were walking along the pavement.

Finally, he said, 'You can't get a cab at this hour. I'll take you home.'

Gone was the bantering humour, the teasing innuendo. It was as if a different man stood there beside her on the pavement, a man who sounded very tired. Well, Julie thought, it certainly didn't take him long to drop the pretence once Lynne and Anita were gone. And that, she added stoutly, was perfectly all right with her.

But she wondered, as he drove her home in a little red sports car, about the sudden change. It wasn't very flattering, she told herself. She had almost let herself believe that he had been attracted to her, that at least a little of his behaviour tonight had been sincere interest.

And who, she asked herself, would want sincere

interest from a man like Greg Roberts? The kind of attention she'd got had been plenty.

She thanked him stiffly for the ride, then stood just inside the bevelled glass front door and watched as the little red car roared off down Grand Avenue. As if, she thought, he couldn't wait another instant to get away.

When Sara came back from her lunch-break the next day, Julie was rearranging merchandise on the built-in sideboard in the dining-room of the old house. Once, it had displayed the treasured possessions of a family, crystal and silver that had been handed down from mother to daughter. Now the precious crystal vases and bowls that lined its carved shelves bore discreet price-tags.

Sara turned a chair around from the huge old table, where an entire service of antique Haviland china was spread out invitingly, as though ready for tonight's dinner party. She sat down and said, 'All right. You've been hiding in your office all morning, and I've been dying for the details. Come on. Where did you meet Greg Roberts? How well do you know him? Is this thing as serious as it looked last night?'

Julie set an antique goblet back on the shelf and straightened a set of monogrammed linen napkins that were nestled invitingly into a half-opened drawer. 'I was not hiding in my office,' she said. 'I was paying the bills.' She stifled the pang of conscience that said it wasn't quite the truth; she'd had every intention of doing her bookwork that morning but, every time she started to write a cheque, Greg Roberts' face had come between her and the paper. It made her furious that he had treated her like that—and even more furious that she hadn't just walked out. Why had she stayed there, and danced with him? It was a question to which she had found no answer, and as a result the bills hadn't been paid, either.

'You're avoiding the question,' Sara pointed out. 'And don't tell me it's none of my business. I know it's not, but I'm your friend—'

'Then, for the love of heaven, Sara, leave me a little privacy and go answer the phone. Last night was nothing important.'

Sara looked troubled. 'You can't spend the evening dancing with Greg Roberts and then shrug it off as if he'd bought you an ice-cream cone.'

'As a matter of fact,' Julie said with wry humour, 'he didn't spend even that much money on me.'

Sara paused in the doorway. 'I really doubt that he's a cheapskate, Julie.' She was back in a couple of minutes. 'Nothing important,' she reported. 'Just a woman who had a garage sale yesterday and thought you might be interested in the leftovers.'

'I wish they'd call me first,' Julie murmured. She draped a pink satin ribbon across a row of unmatched goblets and stepped back to study the effect. 'Some of my best finds are in other people's rubbish, and I could save them the trouble of a sale.'

'That's what I told her, but it didn't sound as if she had anything worth buying to begin with. How long have you known Greg Roberts, anyway?'

Julie sighed. I should have known, she reflected, that a little thing like a telephone call wouldn't have sidetracked Sara's curiosity. She climbed on to a chair and began to dust the row of crystal bowls on the top shelf. 'I had the misfortune of meeting him just last night.'

'You're a faster worker than I thought,' Sara said with admiration.

'And I have no plans to spend any time with him. You won't be tripping over Greg Roberts around here, in case that's what you're hoping for. He won't be coming around, and that's just fine with me.'

Sara looked as if she doubted the truth of that statement, but she didn't argue.

Julie picked up a Bavarian crystal vase. 'Would you wrap this when you get a chance, Sara? A woman bought it while you were out to lunch, and said she'd pick it up tomorrow. It's a wedding gift.'

A wolf-whistle sounded from the doorway, followed by an amused male voice saying, 'Bravo!'

The crystal vase slid from Julie's nerveless hand and shattered against the old oak floor. She twisted around on the chair and glared at Greg Roberts, who was leaning against the door-jamb. 'Dammit,' she said under her breath, and jumped off the chair before he got any ideas about helping her down.

'Watch out for the broken glass,' he said.

'That is not merely broken glass,' she pointed out. 'It is lead crystal, and it's the only vase of that shape that I've ever seen. It retails for eighty-seven dollars.'

He inspected the shards of crystal, gleaming against the mellow wood, and raised grave eyes. 'I don't think it will any more,' he said.

Julie saw red. It was bad enough that she was going

to have to explain this to an irate customer, and refund the woman's money. But the cause of the destruction hadn't even turned a hair, and that made her furious. 'The rule is, if you break it, you buy it,' she said grimly. 'Would you like to pay cash or put it on your charge card?'

'I'm not the one who dropped it.'

'You were certainly the cause of it.'

'I beg your pardon for losing my self-control. I was applauding your slacks, you see. From the back, they fit very nicely.' His amused gaze slid down her body, and he went on, 'As a matter of fact, they aren't bad from the front, either.'

Obviously, she thought crossly, the silence last night when he had brought her home had been only a passing fad. This was the man of early evening, the one who had fed her strawberries and kissed her in the courtyard. 'My slacks are none of your affair.'

'If it walks across my field of vision, Juliet Gordon, it is my business.'

She had bent over to pick up the bits of crystal, but at the caressing note in his voice she stood up straight. He looked quite innocent. 'Sara,' she said, 'I think it would be wise if one of us was in the front of the shop.'

Sara looked regretful. 'She says I won't be tripping over Greg Roberts,' she muttered under her breath. 'And then she kicks me out so I can't.' She slid past Greg and vanished into the old drawing-room.

'You could at least apologise for breaking my vase,' Julie said.

'What happened to the policy of the customer always being right? I came in to browse because my cousin recommended the place, and suddenly I'm being attacked by a virago shopkeeper.'

'You startled me,' Julie muttered.

'Actually, you should expect customers to walk in, you know. Isn't that the point of leaving the front door open?'

'Is there something special you want, Mr Roberts?'

'Oh, several things,' he mused. 'Beginning with you. Between two emerald-green satin sheets, I think. They'd match your eyes.'

'I am not flattered,' she said. 'When a man wants to take a woman to bed at first sight, it doesn't say much for him—his selectivity, or his taste.'

'We're not talking about just any woman,' he pointed out.

That stabbed her to the quick. 'Damn it,' she cried, 'I hadn't seen Keith Evans in five years! I am *not* his mistress. I have no intention of being his mistress. I am not some kind of loose woman—'

He shifted against the door and folded his arms across his chest. 'Funnily enough,' he said, 'I had forgotten all about Keith.'

'I'll just bet you had.' She sniffed once. What was the point? she asked herself. Why get down in the dirt with him?

'Juliet—'

'My aunt is the only person who is allowed to call me that.'

'But it is your name, isn't it?'

'It's on my birth certificate, yes. All the women in my family were named after Shakespeare's heroines.

My Aunt Rosalind and Aunt Miranda insisted that the tradition be continued with me. It's the only grudge I ever held against them. Are you satisfied, or would you like to know where my middle name came from too?'

'What is it? Kate, for the shrew?'

She closed her eyes, took a deep breath, and counted to ten. When she looked at him again, she forced herself to say, politely, 'Is there some merchandise that I can show you? Are you looking for a unique gift, perhaps? Something one-of-a-kind, or personalised?' She saw the gleam start to gather in his liquid brown eyes, and she hurried on. 'Something unbreakable, I'd advise,' she said tartly. 'We have some very nice antique jewellery—'

'I'd like to look around the house,' he said.

'Browse all you like. If you see something you want—'

'I have,' he interrupted.

'I am not for sale.'

He swallowed a smile. 'I meant the house.'

For an instant, she wanted to crawl into one of the cracks between the wide oak boards of the floor. Then gathering anger caught up with her. 'So you're the one who wants to buy the house,' she snapped. That was why he had sought her out last night, she thought. Lynne must have pointed her out, but not for the reason he had implied last night.

'That's right. Why did you refuse to talk to my estate agent yesterday?'

'Because the house is not for sale.'

'Everything is for sale when the price is right.'

'Funny. He said the same thing. It seems to me you both have a few things to learn.'

'I'll give you a hundred thousand dollars today, without even looking at the house.'

'No.'

'A hundred and fifty.'

'Am I to conclude that you want a nice place to live, close to the office?' she asked tartly.

He was silent for a moment. Then he said, gently, 'What I do with it after I buy it is really none of your business, Juliet.'

'Thank you, at least, for not lying to me,' she said. 'Not that it would have made any difference. The house is not for sale, at any price.'

'Perhaps I should talk to your aunt. I understand she owns a half-interest.'

'It wouldn't make the least bit of difference. Randie and I agree.'

'Have you talked to her lately?' Greg asked genially.

'Not in the last few days,' she snapped. 'Have you?'

'No, but I could.'

'Then do so. She'll tell you the same thing I have.'

He smiled. 'Two hundred thousand.'

'I said no. You're only making it more obvious, you know. No one would pay that kind of money for a house without even looking at it unless they planned to bulldoze it.' Her voice shook at the very idea of her house crumbling into a pile of wood splinters, brick dust, and glass shards. 'You've already got the block up the street. What do you want this place for?'

'You really don't expect me to divulge my plans, do you?'

'I'm not going to run out and tell your competition,' she said tartly. 'It wouldn't do them any good, anyway, because whatever you want to build on this property isn't ever going to be done.'

'A quarter of a million. I can have a cashier's cheque for you this afternoon. Two cheques, rather—one for you, one for your Aunt Miranda.'

She looked at him a long time, very thoughtfully. He looked sincere and trustworthy, every inch the responsible businessman in his navy blazer, grey trousers, and open-necked shirt. The formality of last night had given way to casual good taste, but there was no hiding quality. The man probably has his blue jeans tailored, she thought.

But no matter how dependable he looked, she still didn't trust him an inch, and just now she wanted to get away. 'If you'll excuse me, Greg,' she said politely, 'I have to walk my dog. Perhaps I'll see you again some day.' She didn't wait for an answer.

Leicester raised his head with mild interest when she got his leash from the cupboard. He got to his feet as if his arthritic hip was hurting, and padded across to the back door.

'Sometimes I think you don't even need the leash,' she told him as they went down the back steps and the dog turned towards Grand Avenue, 'or me. Your route hasn't varied in ten years.'

The little red sports car started to back out of a spot in the car park next door. There was no point in looking as if she bore a grudge, she decided, and waved a casual hand. The man had made an offer, and she had turned him down. That was the end of it.

The car hesitated and then slid neatly back into the spot. Greg got out and slammed the door, and Julie stifled a groan. Why couldn't I have left well enough alone? she asked herself. He might not have even seen me if I hadn't waved. Why couldn't I have dawdled until I knew he was gone?

'So there really is a dog,' he said cheerfully as he came across the narrow strip of grass that separated the car park from her driveway. 'I thought he was only an excuse for you to vanish into the back of the house and never come out again.' He dropped into step beside her, his jacket pushed back and his hands in his trouser pockets.

'Don't hurt Leicester's feelings. I don't think I'd leave the car there, if I were you. The people who own the car park get a little cranky about my customers parking on their property.'

'Really?'

'You might come back to find that your toy has been towed away.'

He looked over his shoulder at the car and shrugged. 'I think I'll take my chances. Speaking of toys, do you actually drive that collector's item?' He nodded towards the car parked next to the house.

'Certainly I do.' Julie eyed the car appreciatively. The Edsel might have been Henry Ford's only total failure, in production for just two seasons because the car-buying public detested its looks, but she had an aching fondness for it herself. It wasn't the car's fault that it had failed, she often thought. 'The Edsel was a sadly underrated car,' she said. 'It was far ahead of its time, and the public just wasn't quite ready for it. That one has extremely low mileage, too. Rosa bought it new, and only drove it—'

'Don't tell me. To the grocery store, and to church on Sundays.'

Julie laughed in spite of herself. 'It's true, you know.'

'And you let it sit out in the snow and ice? I don't see a garage.'

'No, I put it into storage in the winter and drive Randie's car.' Leicester was tugging impatiently at the leash.

Greg noticed the dog's protest. 'Do you mind if I walk with you?'

'Would it do me any good to object?'

He grinned. 'Probably not. The city council hasn't made a law about that yet, and it is a public pavement. You've got an awfully narrow garden for such a big house.'

'It wasn't that way originally.' She waved a hand towards the concrete car park. 'This was probably the formal garden, when the house was built. It was sold off years ago.'

'It must be unhandy. Where do your customers usually park?'

'In my driveway.'

He eyed the narrow asphalt strip. 'That must be pretty inconvenient.'

'I don't often have hordes of customers all at the same time.'

'No, I can see that.' His tone was thoughtful. He

glanced at his wristwatch, and then at the empty driveway. 'It's only the middle of the afternoon, and there's not a person in sight.'

Julie felt her stomach tightening. 'I do very well, thank you. I have no shortage of customers.'

'Buying gifts? Or do you run another sort of business on the side? At night, perhaps?'

Fury blasted through her bones. 'I see no point in continuing this conversation while you insult me,' she snapped. 'Come on, Leicester. You'll have to make do with a short walk today.' She tugged on the leash. Leicester resisted, his long ears swaying against the cement path. Julie pulled, and Leicester lay down on the pavement, forty pounds of stubborn basset hound.

'Am I going to have to carry you home, you idiot dog?' she asked. Leicester moaned and rolled over at her feet, trembling as if he was in mortal fear.

'Wouldn't it be simpler,' Greg said, 'if you just gave him his normal walk?'

'It would be much simpler, if you would go away!'

'How about if I apologise for implying that you're running a house of ill-repute on the side? I'll take your word for it—your gift shop is a booming business.'

'It's doing very well,' she said stiffly.

'How can you make a living by selling the odd gift?'

'It's more than that,' she said. 'I make it a point to have what no one else in town does—the unusual and the one-of-a-kind. I save people the trouble of being original, and they pay me well for the service.'

'You're certainly original,' mused Greg. When she started to bristle, he put a hand on her arm. 'Don't go off again,' he pleaded. 'I meant it as a compliment, truly I did.'

Leicester took advantage of the slackened leash to start off again on his interrupted walk. Julie followed along without even noticing the route.

Greg sauntered along beside her. 'And that's why the vase you broke costs eighty-seven dollars?'

'That's why.' Leicester padded happily towards the new construction site. 'Shouldn't you be running along?' Julie asked hopefully. 'I can't imagine that walking a dog is your favourite form of entertainment.'

'It isn't. But I'm fascinated, you see. I offered you a quarter of a million dollars for a house a few minutes ago, and you turned it down. I'd like to know why.'

'I don't have to give you any reasons.'

'I know you don't. But I wish you would.' His words were quiet and serious, and the effortless charm was only a minor chord. When she was silent, he sighed and changed the subject. 'A basset hound doesn't seem quite your style,' he observed. 'I'd have expected you to have a Yorkie, or a Pekinese.'

'Leicester was a gift from my Aunt Rosa.'

He looked confused. 'How many aunts do you have?'

She gave up. Obviously, he wasn't going to quit until he understood the whole history of the Gordon family. 'Just two. Rosa—my Aunt Rosalind—and her husband Sid bought this house in the fifties. They never had kids, and Randie—Aunt Miranda—never married, so she came to live with them. Families did that sort of thing then.'

'I know,' he said. 'The big family home, and people moving in and out all the time.'

She nodded. 'Ours wasn't a large family, but this house was the only home we had. I grew up here. My mother died when I was little, and my father travelled with his job, so Randie and Rosa raised me.'

He walked along for a few moments, his stride shortened to comfortably fit hers. 'So, you're turning down financial security so you can cling to the past?'

She was furious. She had satisfied his curiosity, and now he was using the information against her. 'It's nothing like that! I'm not hanging on to the past, I'm preserving it.'

His forehead wrinkled. 'There's a difference?'

'Of course there is. Do you have any idea of the amount of history that's been lost, just in this city, because of people like you?'

'You must realise that you're standing in the way of progress.'

'You may call it progress if you like. I don't believe that you're improving anything by putting up rows of steel rods and acres of faceless glass. Every building you put up rests on the graveyard of a family's history!'

'On the contrary,' he said mildly. 'It provides living space and working space for a great many families.'

'And destroys our cultural inheritance. When your grandchildren ask why you destroyed all those pretty houses on Grand Avenue that they see pictured in the local history books, how are you going to explain to them that profit was worth more to you than aesthetics?'

He scratched his head. 'Since I never intend to have grandchildren, I can't say the problem is keeping me awake nights.'

'There! That's my point. You don't care about future generations.'

'I didn't say that! I just said I didn't plan to contribute to them. And what that has to do with the plans for an office building is beyond me.'

Julie pounced. 'Oh, it's to be an office building,' she said gleefully. 'Well, find someplace else to build it.'

'Why? As long as we're talking of grandchildren, are you keeping this house for yours?'

It stabbed her to the heart, the sudden reminder that she was the last of the Gordons. 'That's really none of your business, Greg. But I'm sure you can understand why I am simply not interested in any offer you might make for my house.'

There was a long silence. Then he smiled down at her. 'Of course I understand,' he said genially. 'It was worth a try.'

Leicester's claws clicking against the tarmac sounded like the fateful ticking of a clock in her brain. No, she told herself. Don't be silly. You've made your point; he's accepted your decision. That's the end of it.

'If you ever change your mind, let me know.' He pressed a business card into her hand and, before she could even look at it, he was gone.

So that's that, Julie, she told herself. There was a strange sort of let-down feeling in the pit of her stomach.

Don't be ridiculous, she lectured herself. You can't possibly be sorry that he gave up so easily.

CHAPTER THREE

JULIE pressed the last strip of transparent tape down against the pale blue foil, and turned the box over to add a crisp silver bow to the top of the package. 'How's that, Mrs Baxter?' she asked.

'It's lovely, my dear. I am so pleased at being able to get a replacement, you know. It nearly broke my heart when I dropped Marian's goblet at her party last week. She was quite understanding, you know; she said that, of course, accidents happen. But an antique crystal goblet like that—I felt I just had to replace it.'

'I'm so glad I happened to have one on hand.' And even more glad, Julie thought, of society's code that says what is broken must be replaced... She glanced at the drawer where the pieces of an expensive Bavarian crystal vase had been resting for the past several days. Greg had been right, technically—she was responsible. But breaking eighty-seven dollars' worth of lead crystal could certainly take the profit out of a day at the gift shop. And it had been his wolf-whistle that had caused the accident, and all her trouble.

It had been a nightmare to explain to the customer who had bought and paid for the vase that she couldn't have it, after all. The woman had said a few choice things about irresponsibility, and it had taken all the firmness and patience Julie could muster before the woman had accepted a crystal bowl worth nearly twice as much as a substitute.

I ought to just throw the pieces away and forget about it, Julie told herself. It's an unpleasant memory, and there is no point in dwelling on it. I'm certainly never going to be paid for the damage; I might as well just write it off as a lesson in business.

She realised abruptly that Mrs Baxter hadn't stopped talking. 'If you'd like to sell it, just let me know,' the woman said.

Her first thought was that Mrs Baxter was talking about the house, and she almost asked if the woman was a friend of Greg Roberts. That's patently unfair, she reminded herself. It had been three days since she'd told Greg that her house was not for sale, and he hadn't bothered her since. Why should she assume that any future question about the house originated with Greg?

Because I don't think he's that easily discouraged, Julie told herself.

'They've bought a big old house on the west side,' Mrs Baxter was rattling on. 'They've never had a formal dining-room before, and they're looking for a sideboard just like that one. So if you'd like to sell the set—'

Relief filtered through Julie's veins. It wasn't the first time someone had tried to buy Aunt Rosa's dining-room set, and she had learned never to say no, even though she would part with her right arm before she sold any of the furniture that Rosa had left. 'I'll think about it,' she said as she rang up the sale and made change.

And a nice little profit that was, she thought as she ushered Mrs Baxter out on to the front step and locked the door. Julie had found that goblet at a yard sale a year ago, covered with dust and filled with rusty safety-pins. Now she had unblushingly sold it for fifty times the amount she'd paid.

She sighed and ran her hands through her hair, tugging it out of the neat twist at the nape of her neck and letting it fall in black waves down her back. She had thought closing time would never come. It had been a long day and, to make it worse, it was Sara's afternoon off. 'I'm ready for a little sunlight,' Julie told Leicester as she started up the stairs to change her clothes. 'How about it? Shall we go play in the garden?'

Leicester made it plain that he would have preferred other ways of spending his afternoon, but he condescended to join her in the walled garden behind the house. If that was the best she had to offer, he seemed to be saying, he'd make do.

It felt good to be outside, soaking up the warmth of the June afternoon. Her shorts and brief top left a good deal of leg bare; Julie wished that she had time to lie outside and work up to a nice golden tan. She wandered around the perimeter of the tiny plot of ground, admiring the lush growth. The bed of day lilies was about to burst into brilliant orange flower, and the summer roses climbed in lavish splendour over the trellises, holding out a promise of riotous colour in the weeks to come. The late strawberry plants were huge, their deep green leaves tinged with red on the edges. It wouldn't be long before the tiny green berries began to form. The thought brought memories of Lynne Hastings' wedding, and of the strawberry Greg had fed her, with that lover's caress…

Don't be an idiot, she lectured herself.

She paused by the wrought-iron gate, her attention drawn by odd noises coming from the car park next door. Surely there shouldn't be anything going on there at this hour? she thought. The business day was done, and the insurance agency had closed.

'You're hearing things, Julie,' she told herself. It sounded like a big truck over there, dropping off steel plates or something just as bulky and heavy. And that made no sense whatever. It certainly wasn't a manufacturing company.

It was one thing to be grateful for, she reminded herself. Her neighbours' businesses were quiet ones.

She cleaned the young weeds out of the bed of lavender and day lilies and debated whether it was too late to set out another tomato plant. It wouldn't produce fruit until fall, but if the frost didn't come till late…

Leicester raised his head from the grass and started to bark. Julie looked at him in astonishment. He seldom barked any more, except when he was playing with Kristen, and this was a rusty, crackly sound, as if he'd almost forgotten how his voice worked.

'Leicester,' she said, 'what's gotten into you? Let's go for a walk.'

For the first time she realised that the afternoon sun was fading quickly into evening. She'd go down to the supermarket, she decided, and pick up a pint of milk and something easy for her supper. Randie would be home some time this week. She'd wait till then to do the full weekly shopping.

Her hand was on the latch of the wrought-iron gate that led out to the driveway when a man appeared just outside it. His white knit shirt was ghostly in the dying light. His sudden appearance startled Julie, and she pulled back into the shadow of the wall. But he had already seen her, so she reluctantly stepped back to the gate.

'What are you doing here?' she asked.

'Snooping,' Greg said cheerfully. 'There was no answer at the front door, so I came around to try the back, and decided to peek into your garden. May I?' He reached over the gate and released the latch to let himself in. 'Nice view back here.'

'If you like brick walls.' Then she realised that he was paying no attention to the garden at all, and an embarrassed flush began at the base of her throat, where the scoop-necked shirt left off, and flooded every inch of exposed skin, till she was bathed in hot colour.

'Yes,' he mused. 'I thought the slacks were very attractive the other day, but the shorts definitely take the honours. I don't suppose you'd turn around for me, if I asked you nicely, so I could admire the back view? No, I didn't think you would. Pity—a woman with a body that gorgeous shouldn't be so self-conscious about it.'

'I am not flattered by your opinions.'

'I know, Juliet. You've already told me that you don't approve of lust at first sight.'

'If you've finished looking, would you like to explain what you're doing here?' There was a challenge in her eyes. She glanced down at the dog, who was growling very softly. 'You're interfering with Leicester's walk again, and he's not very happy with you for making a habit of this.'

'You're going to walk him at this hour?'

'Why not? There's still enough light.'

'Then perhaps I should come along as a bodyguard.'

He looked a little like one tonight, she thought, in his jeans and running shoes and the knit shirt that clung to his muscled shoulders. His hands were on his hips, and the hair on his forearms looked gold in the dim light. I wonder, she thought, if it is as silky as it looks? Then she dragged her thoughts back to safer matters. 'That is why I have Leicester,' she pointed out. 'I don't need another escort.'

'Some bodyguard he'd be! He must be fifteen years old. I'll bet he doesn't even have any teeth.'

'I wouldn't recommend that you underestimate him.'

Greg didn't seem to hear. 'Anything could happen to you on the streets. There might even be vicious dognappers out there, just waiting for a prize like Leicester. I'd better join you, just to be safe.'

'On second thoughts,' Julie said prudently, 'there isn't anything at the supermarket that I can't do without till tomorrow. If you'll excuse me—'

'But I haven't told you what I came for.'

She paused with her hand on the knob of the back door. 'Is there any reason why I should be interested? I haven't changed my mind about selling the house.'

'Not even if we make a trade? We're just finishing

up a condominium complex downtown, with a shopping centre development attached. You could have a condo and a shop—'

She shook her head. 'No, thanks. I'll be spending eternity in a concrete box somewhere—I don't plan to start any sooner than necessary.'

He looked wounded. 'My condos are not concrete boxes.'

'All right, then, glass and steel boxes. It doesn't matter what it's made of; I'm not interested. I like it just fine where I am.'

'You wouldn't even have to go outdoors to get to work.'

She smiled sweetly. 'I don't have to now, either.'

Car headlights flickered through the wrought-iron gate, making a weird pattern of shadows against the garden wall. Julie recognised the fluttery sound of the engine; Miranda Gordon's old Chevrolet sounded remarkably like Randie herself. She shot a look at Greg, trying to decide how best to get rid of him so she could have a private talk with Randie.

There wasn't much of a chance, she decided. Leicester had started to whine happily, and Greg's ears seemed to have perked up at the sound of the engine, too. But it was worth a try. She stooped to pull a last weed in the greying twilight. 'I'll certainly keep your offer in mind,' she said.

'That sounds like a dismissal. Is the person in the car a late customer?' he said brightly. 'Or an early overnight guest?'

Julie threw the weed at him, clinging dirt and all.

'It certainly is none of your business!' she stormed, almost forgetting who was in the car.

He brushed the dirt off his jeans. 'Temper, temper,' he said mildly.

'Juliet?' A door slammed and a quavery voice echoed off the bricks.

'I'm in the garden,' Julie called.

She could almost see the instant when Greg made the connection. 'Aunt Randie,' he said, with an air of self-satisfaction so profound that Julie wanted to hit him.

'Yes, it's Aunt Randie. Now, if you'd like to leave—'

'Why should I do that?'

Julie bit her lip. 'Be a sport, Greg. I'd like to talk to her alone.'

Greg shook his head. 'Oh, no. I want a fair shake in this deal.'

'Juliet?' The gate opened, and a tiny silver-haired woman came in. 'Oh, there you are, dear.' She peered around through thick-lensed spectacles. 'How nice that you asked a friend over to keep you company while I was gone.'

Julie blinked. For an instant, it sounded as if Randie thought she had been gone for an hour or two, and not for nearly a month. I wonder, Julie thought wildly, what she'd say if she really thought I'd had a man staying here with me for the whole three weeks?

Greg stepped forward courteously and extended a hand. 'I'm Greg Roberts, Miss Miranda,' he said. 'I've been looking forward to meeting you.'

Julie put her hand across her mouth to stifle her

giggles. He was treating Randie as if she was a simpering Southern belle, and Julie couldn't wait to see what happened next.

She was disappointed. Randie put her silver head back and looked up what seemed an immense distance, and said, in that gently fluting voice, 'Well, young man, I wonder if you'd help me carry my things in. And then perhaps Julie would fix us all a cup of tea. I could certainly stand something to tide me over till dinner. I've been on the road since early this morning.'

'Randie,' Julie said, with an ominous note in her voice, 'it only takes three hours to drive from Omaha to Des Moines. Where have you been all day?'

Randie laughed, a sprightly little tinkle. 'Oh, Juliet, you know how much I hate those nasty expressways!' She shuddered delicately. 'Everybody goes so fast, and there's nothing to look at while you drive. No towns, and no people—not even many farms, just hundreds of cars, all of them driving too fast. So I just got on the side roads and sort of meandered along, and every now and then there was a little shop, so I'd stop and look. I bought you a few things for the store.'

Julie stifled a groan. Greg heard it; he shot a surprised look down at her.

'Why don't you go on in, Randie?' Julie said. 'Greg and I will get your things.'

'That would be sweet of you, dear. Be careful of the egg crate on the back seat.'

'You brought home a crate of eggs?' Julie croaked. 'Randie, we'll never eat a whole—'

'Of course it doesn't have eggs in it, dear. It was

the only box they had at the little shop where I bought your treasures. You'll stay for tea, Greg?'

Julie jabbed him as hard as she could with her elbow. He let out a surprised grunt, glared at her, and said, 'Of course I will, Miss Miranda. Delighted.'

'Miss Miranda,' Randie repeated, sounding indecently pleased. 'It's been years since anyone called me that. Where did you learn your good manners, young man?'

'Good manners, my left ankle,' Julie growled under her breath. 'Damn you, Greg Roberts.' She raised her voice. 'We'll be there in a minute, Randie.'

Greg opened the back door of Randie's old Chevy and said, 'What is this, a royal progress? How much baggage does one old—' He caught himself, and finished smoothly, 'Do you want to take the treasured egg crate, or shall I?'

Julie peered at it anxiously. 'You can,' she said finally. 'And if you fall and break it, I promise not to complain.'

'Does she do this often?'

'Last trip, it was an entire hand-painted set of china.'

'That doesn't sound bad.'

'The woman who painted it not only wasn't Michelangelo, but there was considerable reason to suspect she was registered blind.'

'Oh.'

'The trip before that, Randie got a bargain on a Victorian horsehair sofa. She shipped it to me collect.'

'And nobody was buying horsehair that year?'

'It's still gathering dust in the attic.'

He reached over the seat to retrieve Randie's keys. The car key stuck in the ignition lock, and when he pulled, the chain disintegrated in his hand. He had to search through the stack of cushions on the driver's seat before he found the last key. 'Does she sit on these when she drives?' he asked, incredulously.

Julie nodded. 'And every two years she toddles down to the examining station, and they renew her licence. She's really not as bad a driver as it looks,' she added, scrupulously fair.

'Well, I now owe her a key-ring,' he said, looking ruefully at the palm of his hand.

'Good. You can pay for your crystal vase at the same time.'

'Not on your life! I wasn't holding that vase when it broke. It was over-priced, anyway. I like value for my money.'

'Is that supposed to explain why you're up to a quarter of a million on this house?' Julie was astounded.

'It's worth it. It's a valuable location. But don't get the idea that I'll go any higher—unless, of course, you'd like to throw your lovely self in on the deal.'

She slammed the door with unnecessary force and started down the drive towards the house, her spine ramrod-straight. She stopped beside the steps, puzzled, and stared across the car park at the insurance agency building, where a truck was drawn up at the front door. 'So that's what I was hearing,' she said. 'They're moving filing cabinets and stuff.'

'That's what it looks like.'

'I wonder why. You don't suppose it's a burglary?'

'Stealing files? What self-respecting burglar would want a bunch of insurance policies?'

'True. But why would they be moving them at all?'

'Perhaps the landlord told them to find another place to do business.' He didn't sound interested.

'There was no landlord. The agent owned the building.' She stared up at him. Under the yellow glow of the street lights, he looked perfectly innocent.

'Just what are you doing here tonight, Greg?' she asked finally. Her voice rose a little. 'Did you just happen by in time to welcome Randie, or was there another reason for being in the neighbourhood?'

He smiled. 'Tell your clients they can use the car park now, if they like,' he offered. 'I don't mind a bit if they park on my property, at least till I decide what I'm going to do with it.'

Miranda Gordon was fussing over the kitchen range when Julie came downstairs. Randie was a strange combination this morning, with her hair wrapped primly in a braid around her head, and a luxurious lacy nightgown peeking out under a serviceable old terry dressing-gown. She had already set the table, and she was banging pans around atop the range. 'My dear, you look as if you haven't slept,' she said. 'Why don't you just go back to bed for a little while?'

'I can't. I have a shop to run, Randie.' How observant her aunt was, Julie thought, with a twinge of irony. She had scarcely closed her eyes all night, after the disaster that had nearly occurred in this very kitchen the evening before—a disaster that Miranda had remained sublimely unconscious of.

It had been bad enough that she had seemed to think, through the entire evening, that Julie had invited this young man home for her aunt's approval. Randie had made it painfully obvious that she approved. That was the problem with Randie, Julie thought. She was so darned anxious to please that she would agree to anything that she thought Julie wanted. Right up to, and including, the sale of the house, which was where the disaster had very nearly occurred.

The concern in Randie's eyes gave way to pleasure as she thought of a way she could help. 'Then, in that case, I'll fix you a nice breakfast to give you strength.'

'Randie, I want a slice of toast, a cup of coffee, and a chance to talk to you. Would you please stop dancing around the kitchen and sit down over here?'

Randie looked at her in astonishment. Julie bit her tongue; never before had she used that tone of voice to her aunt. She said, more gently, 'We really need to talk, Randie.'

Randie sat down at the table and looked at her plate as if she expected it to explode in front of her. 'Oh,' she said, on a note of discovery. 'You want to tell me about Greg!'

'Something like that. Randie—'

'He's a very nice young man,' her aunt assured her. 'Not at all like that—person—who used to come around here.'

'His name,' Julie supplied, 'was Keith.'

'He had no manners at all. I was so happy when you gave him his comeuppance, Juliet.'

Randie, Julie thought drily, had never believed that any man could have the poor taste to jilt her niece.

'But this young man—'

'Is not interested in me,' Julie cut in. 'He is *not* my boyfriend. He's only interested in buying this house.'

Randie looked disturbed. 'Only the house?' she asked plaintively. 'Not you?'

For an instant, Julie wanted to say, *Oh, he'd probably buy me, too, if the price was right.* But that kind of dark humour would only confuse Randie, so she restrained herself. 'That's right. I'm sorry that Greg didn't make himself very clear last night.'

'Oh, but he did!' Randie plunged in anxiously. 'As far as the house is concerned, I mean. And I want you to know that I don't expect you to tie yourself down to this house, Juliet. It's far too big for you to take care of alone, and goodness knows, I'm not much help. I mean, I enjoy puttering around in the kitchen, but that's not the same, is it? And I just don't think it's fair that you—'

Julie broke in ruthlessly. 'Randie, I do *not* want to sell the house!'

'Oh.' Randie looked up, her pale blue eyes magnified by the strong lenses of her spectacles. 'You don't?' she asked helplessly.

'No, I don't. That's why I kicked you under the table last night when Greg started talking about it. I was scared to death that you'd agree to something before we even discussed it.'

'But I thought… It really isn't fair to you, Julie. This house is too much…' Her voice trailed off. 'You don't want to sell it?'

'Of course not. I certainly am not heartless enough to make you move out of your home.'

'Now that I'm in my twilight years, you mean?' Randie murmured, with just a trace of cynicism. 'But it's never really been my home, you know.'

Her voice was so soft that, for a moment, Julie thought she had imagined the words altogether. 'What do you mean? You've lived here for thirty years!'

Randie nodded. 'Yes, but it was Rosa's house, you see. Rosa's furniture. Rosa's things. I was always a guest here.'

Julie was stunned. She had never dreamed that quiet, eager-to-please Randie felt this way. 'Well, it's your house now,' she said robustly. 'And it always will be. If you'd like to move the furniture around, or something—'

'Oh, no. That would interfere with your shop.' Randie smiled absently. 'I'd forgotten that, of course you wouldn't want to give that up.'

'I should say not! Besides, this is a beautiful house. It would be a sin to tear it down.'

'Are you certain he doesn't want to live here? Such a nice young man—'

'That nice young man can't wait to bring the bulldozers in so he can level off this area and put up an office building.'

'I suppose that's progress,' Randie said quietly.

'Not in my book.' Julie gave her aunt an impulsive hug. 'I'm so glad we've had this talk, and decided that we aren't going to sell the house.'

For a moment, it seemed as if Randie hadn't heard. Then she said vaguely, 'Yes, I'm glad, too.'

'Now, I have to go open the shop.' Julie paused in

the doorway. 'I'm sorry. In all the fuss last night, I completely forgot to say welcome home, Randie.'

'Thank you, dear.' Randie picked up the clean plates from the table, carried them across to the sink, and absently deposited them in the dishwater. 'It's nice to be home.'

Julie opened the bevelled glass front door to the early morning breeze. It was already hot but, since there were no customers in sight, she stood on the porch for a few minutes. Across the driveway, a truck bearing a small bulldozer had just pulled in from Grand Avenue, followed by a van. The van doors opened and a crew of men in work-clothes scurried out and vanished inside the empty building that had housed the insurance agency.

'Looks like Greg's not wasting any time,' Julie muttered.

The bulldozer engine roared into life, and she winced at the noise. The operator inched the machine down the ramp and on to the car park, and then leaned forwards in his seat, with his hard hat pushed back. It looked as if he was holding a growling animal on a leash and was uncertain of how much longer he could restrain the impatient beast. The men came out of the building, and one of them made a hand signal to the driver. The bulldozer engine revved to a deafening whine and the machine started to lumber across the ground.

Julie watched the first collision rock the building, its old tile walls shuddering under the impact. She felt as if she had absorbed that blow herself.

The bulldozer backed up and hit the wall again, and it cracked and collapsed upon itself.

'Fascinating to watch, isn't it?' It was almost a yell, and it came from within three feet of her left ear. She jumped and spun around. Greg was standing on her porch. He was wearing jeans again today, topped with a bright yellow hard hat.

'You enjoy destruction, don't you?' she yelled back.

His eyebrows shot skywards. 'Surely you aren't saying that building was an historical treasure?'

'Not exactly,' she admitted.

'I should think not.'

'You're wasting your time and money, you know,' she shrieked. 'Randie agrees with me. This house is not for sale.'

He grinned. 'So you got her buffaloed, did you?'

Julie ignored the accusation. 'There's no point in tearing up the rest of the neighbourhood. You can't build your office tower without this place.'

'It lowers my property taxes if I tear the buildings down,' he retorted.

'That's just the sort of attitude I'd expect from you. Now, if you'd move your car out of my drive, so my customers can get in—'

'They can use my car park.'

'With that bulldozer running around loose? You must be joking! I would never advise them to take the chance.'

'If I were you, I would breathe easier with some cars parked there,' he suggested. 'If the driver of that bulldozer were to lose control and crash into something, I'd prefer it to be a row of cars instead of my house.' He started across the narrow strip of lawn towards the ruined building.

Julie stood stock still for an instant, and then sprinted after him. She grabbed his arm with both hands; his forward momentum nearly threw her off her feet. 'Why, you miserable bastard!' she yelled. 'You're planning to have him drive that machine into the side of my house, and call it an accident?'

'Of course not,' he said. 'I wouldn't plan any such thing. I run a reputable company.'

'Then why did you park your car in my driveway?'

He smiled gently down at her. 'Just in case there's a catastrophe. That's my favourite car.'

'And this is my favourite house! You can't do this, Greg. I'll—I'll sue you for every penny you've got!'

'Of course, Juliet, if such an unfortunate incident were to occur,' he said smoothly, 'I'd be horrified, and terribly sorry about the house. I would instantly volunteer to pay you a generous compensation for the damage my machinery caused. Shall we say—a quarter of a million dollars to ease your pain and suffering?'

She was speechless with fury. She raised her fists, intending to pound them against his chest.

Greg caught her wrists and held her firmly. 'Of course, we all know that money couldn't replace the house. It would have to be torn down immediately so it wouldn't be a danger to you or to the community.'

She was almost in tears. 'You miserable—'

'Yes, I know. You've called me that before. Have a pleasant morning.' He set her aside, touched two fingers to the brim of his hard hat and strode off.

'Stay off my land!' she screamed after him. 'Or you'll regret ever meeting me!'

He turned on the edge of the car park and swept her a bow. 'My dear Juliet,' he said, 'I already *have* regretted it!'

CHAPTER FOUR

JULIE hovered in the drawing-room all morning, moving only when business required. The demand for personalised stationery and antique trinkets was less than overwhelming that morning, and so she had plenty of time to sit in the window-seat, with the lace curtains pulled aside, and watch as the bulldozer made rubble of the old building. Every time the pitch of the motor changed, her heart speeded up another ten beats a minute.

She considered calling the police department, and finally concluded that to do so would only make her look like a fool. There was no doubt in her mind that Greg was working within the law and that he had all the proper permits. What would the police do, anyway? She could scarcely demand that they put an armed guard on her house to keep the bulldozer away! They'd probably drive up, check the paperwork, talk to Greg a minute, and walk off shaking their heads and smiling about the crazy lady next door who thought that some nut was planning to knock her house down. Greg certainly wouldn't admit to having any covert plans.

No, Julie decided, her best protection was to remain inside the house and be highly visible. As long as she sat in the window, she and the house would be safe, because Greg wouldn't take the chance of injuring someone.

'If he did,' she muttered snidely to herself, 'it would cost him a whole lot more than a quarter of a million dollars!'

Randie was walking past the drawing-room door. She paused and then came in. 'Are you talking to me?'

'No. I'm just making noise about the project that's going on next door.' Why bother Randie with the details? Julie thought. She would find it hard to believe that Greg would be capable of that sort of behaviour, anyway. I can hardly believe he'd do it myself. 'But only because it would be so hard for him to get away with,' she added tartly, under her breath.

Randie paused in the bay window. 'I see you're watching your young man. I may be an old woman, but I still know a handsome man when I see one. And that one is mighty good-looking.' She turned around to Julie, her pale eyes suddenly shrewd. 'No comment, hmm?'

'I hadn't noticed.' Julie ducked her head and fingered the loose coral beads in the box of junk she was sorting out. Aunt Rosa had been a collector, and she had never thrown anything away, not even a broken necklace. Some day, Julie thought, someone was going to be looking for a few odd-sized coral beads, and she intended to have just what was needed.

Randie gave a single unbelieving sniff and walked out. Julie's fingers stilled in the box of trinkets, and she leaned her cheek against the cool leaded glass of the window. Across the driveway, Greg was standing with his back to her, broad-shouldered and slim-hipped, watching as the bulldozer began to attack the warren of interior walls in the old building.

Mighty good-looking, Randie had said. Randie had a gift for understatement, Julie thought. Greg Roberts had the stunning variety of good looks that could endanger any woman in his vicinity. I'll bet all he has to do is smile, Julie thought, and hearts break for miles around! Fortunately for her, though, she was immune to that slightly crooked, little-boy smile. And she wasn't impressed by his sincere brown eyes, or charmed by the deep cleft in his chin, either.

Her fingers slid down the glass, as if she was caressing his face, and warm colour bloomed in her cheeks as she remembered the way she had rested in his arms that night in the Botanical Centre's courtyard, when he had kissed her so thoroughly that she had forgotten all about unimportant things, such as the fact that she didn't even know who he was.

Funny, she thought, that it hadn't seemed to matter that night, little things like names…

Well, it mattered now, she told herself with a frown. It mattered a great deal. And she should stop ogling Greg Roberts out of the window and get back to work, or she'd have even more trouble making ends meet next month.

Sara came in about noon like a small whirlwind. 'My gosh,' she said, 'take a day off around here and you never know what you'll come back to find!'

'Well, you certainly won't find many customers lurking in the corners,' Julie warned. 'They see the mess next door and drive on by. I think I'll spend the afternoon in a lawn chair out on the driveway.'

Sara wrinkled her nose in disgust. 'In this heat, and in all that dust, just to see a building torn down?'

'Not quite.' To prevent it, she thought, but she didn't attempt to explain.

'You can do as you like, but I'm staying in where it's air-conditioned. Greg Roberts is out in the kitchen, by the way, talking to Randie.'

Julie was on her feet in an instant.

Sara's eyes were shrewd. 'Have you sold him the house yet?'

'Of course not, and I never will.'

'Then why are you so anxious to see him?' Sara murmured.

'Because he's talking to Randie.'

'Does that mean she's sensible enough to listen to him?'

'Sara, just run the shop, all right? Leave the management decisions to me.'

'Does that mean that Greg Roberts is also your affair?' She grinned slyly. 'Well, some of us are luckier than others.'

'Sara—'

'Yes, boss,' Sara said, in a voice that sounded much meeker than it was. 'I'll get my dust-cloth out right now. Or is that a management decision, too?'

Greg was drinking coffee at the kitchen table, his yellow hard hat and leather gloves laid aside. There was a fine sheen of dust on his dark curls where the hat hadn't protected it. He looked up at Julie and smiled, and her heart rocked just a little. It wasn't fair, she thought, for a man to be so damned sexy that even when he was covered with plaster dust he was enough to make a woman lose her head.

He glanced at his wristwatch and murmured to Randie, 'I think she's checking on us. I've been here exactly five minutes.'

Randie giggled like a lovestruck teenager, and Julie's spine stiffened. 'I merely came out to fix my lunch,' she explained haughtily.

'I have a better idea. It's too noisy to hear yourself think around here—'

'Whose fault is that?' she muttered.

'So why don't I take you ladies out to lunch?'

Randie fluttered over with the coffee-pot and refilled his cup. 'Oh, that would be lovely, Gregory,' she said, 'but I just don't want to go out in the heat. You young people go and have a good time.'

He raised an enquiring eyebrow at Julie, who said, 'No, thank you. I've planned my lunch already.'

'But Juliet!' Randie was shocked. 'I've looked in the refrigerator, and there is simply nothing worth eating in there. You can't possibly—'

'Randie,' Julie said firmly. 'Don't you need to go call someone?'

'Who, dear?'

'Anyone.' There was a world of meaning in the single word.

Randie blinked. 'Oh. Of course, dear. Have a good time—' She vanished up the back stairs.

Greg smothered a smile and said, 'If you were trying to convince her that you can't stand me, that was a tactical error.'

'I really don't care what Randie thinks, all right?'

'That's rather obvious. You didn't even consult her about selling the house—instead, you told her. Where shall we have lunch?'

She looked him over, from dusty hair to boots that looked as if they had been dredged in powdered cement, and said, 'What have you got to offer? I suppose we could get a sandwich at the corner delicatessen and sit on the pavement to eat, but frankly I'd rather have tuna salad at home where it's cool.'

'Are you telling me that you don't think I could get into a decent restaurant?'

She thought about it, and decided that, if Greg Roberts showed up at the door, any restaurant in town would suddenly have a lapse of memory concerning the dress code. 'In any case,' she said, 'it doesn't matter. I have no intention of leaving my house as long as your bulldozer is next door. You probably only want to get me out of here so the accident you've planned can happen on schedule.'

He frowned a little. 'I really would like to talk to you.' The humour had died out of his voice.

'So talk.' She put her head in the refrigerator and decided that Randie had been right; there was nothing worth eating.

'Without the possibility of Randie overhearing.'

Randie popped her head around the corner. 'Oh, are you two still here?' she asked brightly. 'I thought you'd be in a hurry to go—lunch hours are so short, you know.'

'I know,' Greg said, with a stunning smile. He pushed his chair back. 'That's why we've decided to pass on lunch, and have dinner together tonight instead.'

Julie stood up without remembering where she was, and banged her head against the refrigerator shelf. The impact brought tears to her eyes.

'Oh, that's a lovely idea,' Randie said. 'I'm sure you'll enjoy yourself more, Juliet. I'm sure he'll take you somewhere just wonderful.'

'I shall,' Greg promised lightly. 'I'll pick you up at about seven, Julie. Until then…' He captured her hand and raised it to his lips.

From where Randie stood, Julie thought, it must have looked like a courtly gesture. But then Randie couldn't see his tongue darting along the lifeline in Julie's palm, and caressing the sensitive skin between her fingers. She knew he was waiting for her to protest, and she bit her lip to keep from uttering the sharp words. There were mischievous devils dancing in his eyes.

She sighed. With Randie standing right there, what could she say? I can slip out a little later, she thought, and tell him that I wouldn't go to dinner with him tonight even if I was handcuffed and dragged. But, in the meantime, why cause any more trouble with Randie? 'Until then, make sure that bulldozer stays on your side of the property line,' she warned. 'I'll be watching.'

'Observing the bulldozer?' he murmured. 'Or me?'

Less than an hour later, blessed silence descended on Grand Avenue. The bulldozer had snarled its way back aboard the truck and had been hauled away, leaving a mountain of rubble. The next time she looked out, Greg had vanished too.

Julie thought about it all afternoon, and decided not to make a production out of refusing to have dinner with him. After all, she thought, what did she have to lose? She'd said no to the man a dozen times already; it couldn't be any harder to say it again. If he was foolish enough to believe that buying her dinner was enough to change her mind, let him pay the bill. It would be all he would get for his efforts.

Besides, she thought, trying to get rid of a man like Greg Roberts, who had probably never had an ounce of trouble in attracting the women he wanted, might only encourage him to try harder.

Randie was in the sitting-room at the end of the wide upstairs hallway, needlepointing a new cover for a chair Julie had picked up at a garage sale, when Julie came out of her bedroom. 'How nice you look, dear,' she said.

Julie spun around, enjoying the soft swish of the jersey skirt of her favourite red sundress. Her long, dark hair bounced against her shoulders, tickling the bare skin, and her strappy red sandals made her feel elegant. It was nice, she thought, to be going out with a man who was so much taller that it didn't matter how high her heels were. Julie was five feet nine in her stockinged feet. In any kind of heel, she'd been taller than Keith, or most of the other men she'd dated.

'But surely you're not going to wear the jacket?' Randie fretted. 'You've such pretty shoulders, Juliet; you shouldn't cover them up with that garish print.'

Julie glanced down at the bright geometric-printed

jacket that lay across her arm. 'He didn't tell me where we were going.' With the jacket, the dress could go anywhere. And, if it turned out to be one of the more formal restaurants, she could take the jacket off and leave her shoulders and throat bare.

'He'll want to show you off. Where did you get those jet ear-rings?'

'At a flea market a couple of weeks ago. I borrowed them from the shop.' Julie tossed her head, and the long, coal-black drops sparkled briefly and then settled back to half hide in her long hair.

'You should have pretty things of your own, Juliet.'

'I can't afford to. It's a vice, and if I once started, I'd bankrupt myself.'

Randie was not amused. 'It's not a vice, exactly,' she mused. 'It's a natural wish. I had a jet necklace once. What happened to that? I wonder if it's still in my jewellery case.'

'Don't knock yourself out to find it. Some of them are pretty awful.'

But Randie had laid her needlepoint aside, and disappeared to her room. Julie perched on the window-ledge and looked down at the heap of rubbish that had been the building next door.

'How all that plaster and brick and concrete could have come out of that one small building is beyond me,' she said as Randie returned.

'Gregory will clean up the mess, I'm sure.'

Julie was in much better spirits now that the bull-dozer was gone. 'I don't care what he does,' she said magnanimously, 'as long as it's quiet over there. If he doesn't haul it away, I'll go plant morning glory all the way around it and let the vines cover it up.'

Randie made a noise that might have been agreement. 'Here's the necklace.'

Julie stretched out a hand and caressed the elaborately carved and faceted beads. 'Randie, it's beautiful! Do you know what something like this is worth? Why didn't you ever show it to me before?'

'Because you knew what it was worth,' Randie said drily. She held the necklace out of Julie's reach. 'If I give it to you, Juliet, you must promise that you won't sell it.'

'Darling, you know that I've sold very few family things.'

'I didn't mean that you should keep it because it was mine, but because it's exactly right for you. That is worth far more than the monetary value of the jet.' She draped it around Julie's throat. 'Wear it in love, my dear.'

Julie brushed a gentle finger across Randie's petal-soft cheek. 'I will, Randie.' She glanced out of the window again. 'Oh, there's Greg.' She jumped up, seized her jacket and the red handbag that matched her shoes, flew down the stairs and opened the front door before he could reach for the bell.

'That was prompt,' he said. He gave her a questioning glance as she pulled the door shut behind her. 'Don't I have to be inspected?'

'By Aunt Randie? Of course not; I'm a grown woman. Besides, it's not as if this was a date, exactly.'

He grinned. 'Does that mean she isn't going to be waiting up for you, either?'

'Don't get any ideas.'

'I promise not to get any new ones, at least.' He helped her into the car.

He took her to a private club atop one of the new buildings downtown. 'We built this,' he offered as the sleek elevator swept them to the top floor. 'If you'd like to look at the condos I told you about—'

'No, thanks.'

'Now don't go all prim and proper on me. I wasn't making a pass at you.'

'I simply meant that I didn't want to waste your time. I am not interested in a condo.'

'Living in one would have advantages for you.'

'Name one.'

'There's a parking ramp,' he pointed out. 'You wouldn't have to store your car in the winter.'

'I've managed for a good many years.'

'Yeah. Well, what about Randie? If she had a fall on the icy driveway—'

'She doesn't drive in the winter, and I don't want to encourage her to start.'

'Does that mean she just sits in the house and waits for spring to come?'

It made Julie uncomfortable; he had a way of taking the facts and twisting them ever so slightly, till it sounded as if Randie was imprisoned. It isn't like that, Julie wanted to say, but she knew it would do no good.

The dining-room was large but uncrowded. 'It's one of the things I like best about this club,' Greg said. 'It's a wonderful place to do business, because the tables are so far apart that you can't be overheard unless you're shouting.'

'Is that a warning?'

'I don't know. Were you planning to shout? Would you like a drink?'

'Just a Bloody Mary. And I'll shout only if you are unreasonable.'

'I am never unreasonable.' He ordered her drink and a Scotch and water for himself, and leaned back in his armchair, looking around with satisfaction. 'I think we did rather well here, actually.'

Julie shrugged. 'If you like modern glass and steel.'

'If you want old buildings, Juliet, go to Europe.'

'Just how do you think they got old?' Her Bloody Mary was tart and cold. She sipped it and said, logically, 'Really, Greg, if you would just understand that there is no way we'll ever agree on this thing, and it's pointless to pursue it—'

'That's probably true,' he mused. 'And I'd rather pursue you, anyway.'

'That was *not* what I meant.'

He reached for her hand. She moved it, trying to make it look casual. His eyes twinkled wickedly. 'I forgot to ask you what Randie brought home in the egg crate last night.'

Julie rolled her eyes. 'The most awful assortment of pressed glass you'll ever see in one place.'

'Junk?'

'Not all of it. She accidentally picked up a few pieces that were marvellous.' Her fingertips caressed the jet necklace, and she felt ashamed of herself. 'I shouldn't underestimate Randie—she does occasionally have flashes of wonderful taste.'

His eyes rested on the black beads that hid the hollow at the base of her throat. 'That's beautiful,' he offered.

'Thank you. It was Randie's.'

'Your throat?'

'The necklace, you idiot!'

'Oh. That's nice, too, but I was admiring...' He raised a hand to caress the satin skin.

She leaned back in her chair to escape his warm fingers. 'Look, Greg,' she said, 'I really do not want to spend the evening wrestling with you—'

'Sorry,' he said. 'I just can't help myself, you know. I've felt this way since that night at the Botanical Centre—as if I just can't keep my hands off you. I know, you're going to say that you're not flattered. Well, you should be.'

'You don't know me very well.'

He put an elbow on the table and propped his chin on his palm. He looked, she thought, just a little like Leicester did when he smelled a steak cooking and knew that he couldn't have it. 'So, tell me what I ought to know about you,' he said.

He only wants to find out where your weaknesses are, she told herself. But even through her suspicions, she found herself responding to his questions. She told him about what it was like as a child to live with Rosa and Randie, about her brief time at the university, about the way she had come to start Exclusively Yours—about everything except Keith.

'If you hadn't quit school,' he said, as they finished the Châteaubriand, 'what would you have done?'

'I was thinking of being a lawyer.' It had been at a law students' party that she had met Keith. It was the first time she remembered it with sadness, and not with guilt and anger.

'Do you ever regret not doing it?' It was a gentle question, and it was impossible to take offence at it.

'Not really. I like retail sales, and I really enjoy being my own boss.' Then a challenging light came into her eyes. 'Except for the last few days. If I'd had that diploma on my wall this morning, you would have been served papers.'

He shook his head. 'You've got no grounds. I'm not doing anything illegal. I owned the building and I tore it down, within the limits of my official permits.'

'How about threatening to knock down my house?'

'I didn't do anything of the sort. You jumped to conclusions, so I just saw how far I could lead you on. Look, Julie, it really hurt my feelings that you had no more faith in my integrity than that.'

'If you could have gotten away with it,' she said drily, 'you'd have done it.'

He looked wounded, and she didn't have the heart to pursue it further. Mention of the house had shattered the magic mood, and suddenly she wanted desperately to find the way back to that easy companionship.

'Tell me about you,' she said softly.

'What do you want to know?'

She sipped her wine. 'Did you break all your toys when you were a baby,' she teased, 'or is demolition a new interest?'

'That's not fair,' he complained. 'You have to give me credit for the things I build, too.'

'I just don't understand,' she said. She drew an intricate pattern on the linen tablecloth with the tip of her fingernail. 'I know a little about your family—every kid in this state reads about the early settlers. Your great-grandparents, and mine, homesteaded this prairie. They came out here in covered wagons and broke the sod with walking ploughs. Isn't that important to you? Don't you appreciate your heritage?'

'You forget that they occasionally tore down a settler's abandoned cabin, too. If no one ever destroyed, how could we build?'

'That's different.'

'In what way? If you really want to be a stickler, Julie, you should be screaming about the thousands of acres of prairie grass that are gone—covered by farmland and highways and towns. That grass was here for a great many more years than the houses you're crying about, and it was just as much a treasure to this state. It helped to produce the black topsoil that we're exploiting now.'

The waiter brought the dessert tray around. Julie chose the bombe Italienne, and waited until the waiter had set the frothy, frozen confection before her. She drew lines in the whipped cream with the tines of her fork, and said, her voice troubled, 'But that was necessary, Greg. They had to make a living—'

'So do the people who live here now. Sometimes idealism and reality just don't mix, Julie.'

'I know that sometimes history has to give way. But isn't there the tiniest bit of idealism in you?' she challenged. 'Don't you ever do anything that's the slightest bit impractical, just because it feels right? Or do you always have everything plotted out?'

His smile started in his eyes, she realised, and only

after the twinkle burned brightly there for a moment did it reach his mouth. He really was quite shockingly attractive, she thought. Perhaps she wasn't immune, after all. That little-boy smile alone was threatening to destroy the rational part of her brain.

'You have tunnel vision, Juliet,' he murmured, 'if you really think that about me.'

'Well, Greg,' said a woman's voice, 'if I'd seen you earlier, hiding in the shadows, I'd have invited you to join us.' Under the cultured tones, the voice was strident.

Greg rose slowly. 'Hello, Anita. Keith. You met Julie at Lynne's wedding, I'm sure.'

'No one met her,' Anita purred. 'You kept her very effectively sewed up all evening, Greg. One must wonder why.' Her eyes were vicious.

Julie's heart was pounding so hard that she thought her chest would explode. My God, she thought, Anita knows about me. Did Keith tell her? Why would he have done such a thing? Surely he doesn't still think that I could ever want him back!

He hates Greg, she realised. Keith was smiling, but his eyes were hard as he politely shook hands. There was a repressed fury about him.

He doesn't know how transparent he is, Julie thought. There was a bit of relief in that; perhaps Keith hadn't said anything to his wife at all. It wouldn't take much intuition for Anita to guess what was in his mind, that was sure.

Greg said lazily, 'I didn't want anyone trying to steal her from me—that's why I was so careful of her that night. Don't let your dessert melt, darling.' His hand rested solicitously on Julie's bare shoulder, sending waves of warm strength through her body. There was a command in his touch, as well, and she responded to it automatically.

'It was very nice to see you again,' Julie murmured.

Dismissed, Anita and Keith had no choice but to move on across the dining-room. Greg watched them out of the corner of his eye; he looked relaxed, but Julie could feel the tension there. Only when the elevator had swept the couple away did he lean back in his chair. He scooped up his wine glass in lazy fingers, and she could feel the weight of his gaze.

'That was rough,' she breathed. 'Thanks for defending me, Greg.'

'Sometimes,' he said, 'I wonder if I'm an utter fool.'

She glanced up at him, and was stunned to find none of the customary humour in his gaze. Instead, there was wary distrust, and her eyes fell in confusion. What now? she thought. Surely he can't still think that Keith and I...

But he might, she realised. Heaven knew what sort of gossip he'd heard, and she had made no move to clarify things. Suddenly, it was very important to her that he know the truth, even if it made him think she was a moron.

She took a deep breath. 'I lived with Keith for two years,' she said. Her voice was low and hard, but it could not conceal the pain she still felt whenever she thought about what an ingenuous fool she had been. 'I quit school and worked two jobs to help pay his law school tuition. Whenever his parents were in town, I moved out—he said they were prudes and wouldn't understand that we loved each other so much that conventions weren't important.'

He shifted uneasily in his chair, and said, 'Julie—'

She went on, ignoring him, knowing that if she once paused to consider what she was saying, any composure she had would crumble. 'A month before he graduated, I picked up the Sunday newspaper and read his engagement announcement. That was the first hint I had that he'd been dating Anita while I was at work. I—' Her voice broke, and she steadied it with an effort. The black pain of betrayal that had swamped her that day had felt as if she'd been suddenly encased in lead; it had left her unable to move, unable to think—able only to breathe, and to wish that she could stop that, too, and be released from her misery.

'Julie,' he said. 'You don't have to tell me this.'

She wasn't listening. 'I moved back home with Rosa and Randie that afternoon,' she went on quietly, in a voice that quavered. She hadn't cried, she remembered. It was too terrible an agony to be healed by tears. She had walked around for weeks in a sort of dazed uncertainty, and when she had begun to feel again, there had been nothing left but cold anger—at Keith for using her, and at herself for being so gullible.

'I didn't see him for five years, till Lynne's wedding. I never want to see him again.'

Please, she thought desperately, you have to understand, Greg, just how awful it was. You must understand.

There was a long silence. Greg sat motionless, his wine glass dangling between two fingers.

'He isn't important to me,' she said. 'Not the way—'

Not the way that you're important, she thought, and was suddenly breathless at the impact of the realisation.

Greg set the glass down. 'Let's go,' he said. He didn't look at her, and she had no way of knowing whether he had believed her. Whether, indeed, it even made any difference.

Why should it matter to him? she asked herself. Don't jump to conclusions, Julie. Just because you've suddenly realised that you could grow to like him far too much for your own good, that doesn't mean he feels the same way about you.

In the mirrored elevator, she leaned into the corner and closed her eyes, unwilling to look at him. If there was pity in his eyes, or anger, or embarrassment, she couldn't handle it. She would rather not know.

It was only a few blocks from the sleek tower to the old house on Grand Avenue, and traffic was so light that in a matter of minutes the little red sports car pulled into her driveway. Julie reached for the door-handle and tried to mumble her thanks. Greg's door slammed on her words, and he came around to help her out of the car.

'I enjoyed dinner,' she said. 'I—'

'I'm coming in.' His tone was low, expressionless, factual.

She was startled and half panicked. 'Why?'

'Because I can't kiss you properly in a sports car with bucket seats, that's why.' He sounded impatient, as if she should have figured that out for herself.

'But—' She stumbled on the gravel, and his hand jerked her upright.

'Keith is an ignorant twerp, and I don't care to waste any more time on him.' He took the key from her hand and unlocked the big door. 'Can we go in here?' He indicated the wide doorway of the old drawing-room.

'Yes. I—I don't understand—' She groped for the light switch. He caught her hand, and pulled her into his arms, and Julie tensed. 'If you think that because I lived with Keith I'm anxious to go to bed with just anyone—'

'I am not just anyone,' he said unsteadily, with his lips pressed against the hollow at the base of her throat. 'If you need proof that I'm a gentleman, remember that I did bring you home. Randie is upstairs, so with one good scream you could have the cavalry on its way to rescue you. Julie—'

His mouth was gentle against the satin skin. Ripples of wonder raced through her at the soft caress.

'But you're not going to scream, are you?' he whispered against her lips.

'No...' she breathed, and his mouth came down hard on hers, demanding, searching, seeking. His tongue teased against her lips, and Julie relaxed against him and let him explore the soft mystery of her mouth, sending a lightning storm of sensations surging along every nerve. One of his hands was tangled in her hair; the other crept along her spine, pressing her so closely against him that her toes were the only bit of her that still made contact with the ordinary world. She couldn't breathe—she didn't *want* to breathe, because it might break the bond between them.

Greg began to plant tiny, moist kisses over her face and down her throat. The strap of her dress slid down over her shoulder, and his mouth brushed the gentle curve at the top of her breast. Her head fell back as if the muscles that held it had been cut. The heat of his hands kindled a blaze that no fireman could fight, a flame that threatened to sweep away everything except her longing for him.

'I want to kiss every inch of you like this,' he said huskily. 'I want to love you till you scream for mercy, and then start from the beginning again.'

She tried to open her eyes. She should put an end to this, she thought dimly. This was supposed to be a goodnight kiss, not a one-act seduction…

'Come home with me tonight, Julie.' He feathered kisses across her cheekbone, kissed her earlobe, traced the outline of her ear with the tip of his tongue.

'I can't,' she croaked. 'Randie—'

'You're a grown woman,' he reminded her. 'Leave a note for Randie. I'm sure she'll understand.'

'That's more than I do,' she whispered. 'Greg, I don't know what's happening to me.'

'Yes, you do. You want to make love with me just as much as I want you. It's simple.'

'But it isn't!' she cried. 'It's too soon! Please—'

He pulled back a fraction of an inch. 'What do you mean, too soon? I've wanted you like this since the moment I saw you. And don't tell me that you don't want me, Julie. I don't believe you.' He pulled her even closer against him, and the ache inside her grew.

'Greg, I've only started to know you. It's just been a few days, and half the time we've been like enemies.'

'This is a good way to get acquainted,' he growled playfully against her throat. But she didn't smile, and after a moment he sighed and let her go. 'All right. If it's important to you to wait, I'll go home alone to a cold shower.'

The sudden loneliness of being apart from him nearly made her throw all sense to the winds. I want to go with him, she thought.

'Will you at least kiss me goodbye?' he said, very softly. 'And give me a promise that soon—very soon—'

I should stay away from him, she thought, and found herself moving back into his arms. 'Oh, why did the house have to get in the way?' she said, more to herself than to him.

He held her a fraction of an inch from him, and said, 'Sell it to me, Julie, and then it won't be in the way any more.' His mouth moved greedily across the hollow of her cheek and down to caress the stubborn line of her jaw. 'You will eventually, you know. Let's settle it now and have it over with. Come and stay with me.'

The words sank into her conscious mind like a lead weight into a shallow pool, and she remembered wondering just that afternoon if his invitation had been planned as a way to soften her opposition. But I never thought he'd go so far, she cried out in inner anguish. It was bitter agony to keep her voice even. 'Oh, you'd like that, wouldn't you?'

'Sounds like a lot of fun to me.' He grinned down at her and kissed the tip of her nose.

She struggled, as much against her own desires as to get away from him. 'Let go of me! So that's what all this was about? You do a good act, Greg Roberts!' She was fighting tears. 'You nearly had me convinced that I was the most fascinating woman you've ever met, and that you'd thoroughly enjoy taking me to bed. I don't doubt you would have done it, too.' She aimed a kick at his shin.

'Julie!' He let her go abruptly.

'Well, for your information, I am not interested in trading my house for a romp in your bed. I will never give up my house, no matter what I have to do to keep it! I would sooner sell my body on the street than let you take what is mine. Get out and stay out, and don't bother me ever again!'

There was a long and tormented silence. She had turned her back on him and stood with her fists clenched, her knuckles pressed against her teeth to keep from crying out with the pain that tortured her. She pulled the strap of her dress impatiently back into place.

He moved then. He reached over her shoulder and thrust something with sharp edges down into the shadow between her breasts. She jumped and cried out, and he let his hand linger in a rough caress, his fingers splayed across her breast.

'So you'd sell yourself on the street,' he mused. 'Well, put that on my account. It should buy me a reasonable bit of your time and talents. And remember, when you get ready to start your new business, that I am first in line.'

The door slammed behind him. When she heard the car start, she crept out to the hall and turned the big brass lock. Her whole body was trembling as if she had a fever.

The sharp edges of the object scratched her breasts, and she pulled it out. It was a crumpled hundred-dollar bill, and it seemed to burn her hand.

Julie threw it as far as she could.

CHAPTER FIVE

IT'S too hot to sleep, Julie told herself at three in the morning. Air-conditioning was fine in its place, she decided, but the air that it recirculated seemed stale and dead. And it was too hot to open the windows. That would only bring in steamy, humid air, still baking in the heat that had been absorbed by the concrete all day.

It's the humidity that makes it really uncomfortable, she decided at four o'clock, as she tossed her hair against the damp pillow. Everything seemed to be sticky because of it. She got up and stood under a cool shower for a few minutes, then left her silky pyjamas in a heap on the carpet and got back into bed. The sheets slid sensually over her naked body, reminding her of the way Greg had held her. She closed her eyes and pulled her pillow over her face.

'Oh, at least be honest with yourself,' she muttered irritably at five o'clock, when sleep still was a stranger. It wasn't the weather that was keeping her awake, but the heat of her own thoughts. If Greg was here, she lectured herself, beside you in this bed, you wouldn't give a thought to the temperature.

And she wished—oh, how she wished!—that she had not remembered that he wanted to buy her house. Then she could have gone with him, she could have celebrated the astounding way she felt about him.

That way, you wouldn't have been reminded of it till morning, she told herself sternly. Until the matter of the house was settled, how could she believe that he felt anything for her at all? He must have tons of money invested in this project, and she alone was standing in the way. How could she trust anything he said?

She dropped into an uneasy doze at six, and was awakened before seven by a jarring thud that brought her upright and to the window before her eyes were even open.

The thud, she realised, bleary-eyed, had been caused by an endloader as it bounced off a ramp from truck to car park. She put her hand to her temple, where a headache already throbbed, as the machine's engine started up.

'Randie should thank heaven that her bedroom is on the other side of the house,' she muttered to herself. She lay down again, but the roar of the endloader as it gathered the rubble into piles was incessant. When the first dump truck pulled into the car park, jouncing over the kerb with a nerve-shattering crash of metal, Julie gave up. There would be no rest.

Early as it was, the heat was already nearly unbearable. Even inside the air-conditioned house, the air seemed sticky and heavy. Julie put on a lightweight cotton dress in a royal blue and aqua paisley print, considered whether tights were really necessary, and jammed her bare feet into sandals instead. She had just started the coffee when the back doorbell rang.

She looked up and froze at the sight of a tall figure on the steps. Greg, her heart cried. He came back—

Then she swallowed hard. Because he still wants the house, she reminded herself. She pulled the door open. 'I told you not to bother me again,' she accused.

His face was hard. He held up a scrap of bright, geometric fabric, holding it between two fingers as if it had a noxious smell. 'I wouldn't have, except that you left this in the car last night. I didn't think you'd hesitate to accuse me of stealing it, so I brought it back.' He dropped the jacket into her hand.

'You're not wearing your hard hat,' she observed. 'Does that mean you aren't tearing anything down today?' He was wearing charcoal trousers and a muted plaid sports coat.

'Not exactly. I'm only checking in at the sites today, before I go to the office.'

'The men can make enough of a mess without your help, is that it?'

His jaw tightened at the taunt, but he replied civilly. 'I employ good men, and I trust them. But I always like to be on hand when the dozer's running.'

'Just in case of accident?'

'Something like that. You look awful this morning.'

'Thanks,' Julie snapped.

'Didn't you sleep well?' The false solicitousness in his voice made her want to double up her fist and put it through his teeth.

'Your damned endloader woke me up this morning. Must you start rattling the neighbourhood at this hour?'

'Seven o'clock is scarcely the middle of the night. We're human too, you know; my men like to avoid the heat.'

'Then why don't you take your entire company to Alaska?'

'Because I have too much money at stake to leave here.' The words were bitten off, as if he was restraining himself.

'Is that a threat?'

'No, it's an announcement. I've invested too much in this project to stop now.'

'I am not interested in whether you lose your money.'

'Juliet, I still plan to build this office complex.'

'What a pity that you didn't arrange to buy all the land first,' she said sweetly.

Greg went on as if she hadn't interrupted. 'But if I can't do that,' he said, 'there are other uses for the property I own. There's a printing company looking for a new place to build. I'm sure you'd enjoy having presses running round the clock, and trucks unloading paper in the wee hours of the morning.'

She looked critically over his shoulder. The end-loader dumped a bucketful of rubbish into a truck. The resulting cloud of dust rolled across the car park and slammed into the garden wall. 'It isn't big enough,' she said.

Greg grinned without humour. 'Oh, didn't you know that I own the lot behind you, and also the one on the other side of your house? I could build in a U-shape right around you, Juliet. Tell me, would you like dumpsters at your back door and air-conditioning units lining your garden wall?'

She refused to be intimidated. 'There are laws against that sort of thing.'

'I know. It requires careful planning to circumvent them. I figure you're going to be stubborn long enough for me to devise blueprints that no zoning board will argue with.'

'Threats are not going to make me sell, Greg, any more than your misguided persuasion did last night.'

His face seemed to darken, and a nerve twitched in his cheek. 'If you had gone to bed with me,' he said, 'the house would have had nothing to do with it.'

'No,' she agreed placidly. 'I'm sure you would have arranged to enjoy yourself. Whatever else you are, Greg, you're certainly not a martyr.'

His jaw muscles tightened, and for a moment, she thought she had gone too far. 'I wish I'd dealt with your Aunt Rosa,' he said.

'Yes, that would have made it easier, wouldn't it? Unfortunately, Rosa's been dead for two years, and you're dealing with me.'

'I could have offered her a life interest,' he said thoughtfully. 'She could have lived here as long as she liked, and I'd have gotten the place when she died. But you—'

He looked her over at length, his eyes dark and moody. Julie stood her ground, trying to stifle the shivers that wanted to cruise up and down her spine. He was inspecting her as if she was a steel beam, she thought—one that had just been found to have a serious flaw—not as if she was human at all.

'You look a little too healthy to make that sort of deal worth my while,' he went on.

'It would be foolhardy of me to agree to it,' she said, catching her breath with an effort. 'I'd be looking over my shoulder all the time, expecting Jack the Ripper to be sneaking up on me.'

'Of course,' Greg mused, 'sexually frustrated women don't generally live as long—and you've got to be one of the most thwarted old maids in this city.'

'Why, you—'

'You're afraid to take a chance, and afraid to look forwards instead of back. By the way, I've changed my mind about letting your customers use my car park.'

'I had no intention of becoming indebted to you.'

'The men are going to begin breaking up the concrete this morning. The cement saws will start as soon as the endloader finishes with the building rubble. Enjoy yourself, Juliet. It may be a long and unpleasant summer.'

She was standing there with her mouth open when he left. The screen door hit the frame behind her, and bounced open again just as the endloader dropped another bucketful of rubble. Dust billowed up from the dump truck and whirled across the driveway, and Julie got a mouthful of the bitter, chalky cloud. She choked and tried to spit it out, but it seemed to absorb every drop of moisture in her mouth and throat.

Damn him anyway, she thought. The vindictive monster! Calling me an old maid...

'Perhaps that's what you are, Julie,' she told herself.

She ignored the coffee, steaming gently in the glass pot, and went into the front of the house. Without looking at the title, she pushed a cassette into the tape deck that provided background music for the shop. The relentless symphonic beat of water against rock filled the room; Rachmaninov's *The Isle of the Dead*, she reflected, was quite appropriate for her mood this morning. She'd like to play it at Greg Roberts' funeral! She sat down on the high stool behind the cash register, and started to sort money out of the bank bag into the drawer.

'Julie!' a little soprano chimed. 'I came to work with Mommy today.'

Julie looked up with a smile. It was hard to be gloomy with Kristen around, she reflected. Funny that in the last few days the longing for a child of her own had diminished. In fact, she realised, she hadn't even thought about it in a couple of days. 'I see, poppet. What brings you in?'

Sara groaned. 'My baby-sitter decided just yesterday that she wanted to take a vacation over the Fourth of July. I thought that if I asked for another day off this week, you'd kill me. Therefore, I brought the kid along.'

'You know she's no problem.' Julie gave Kristen a hug.

'Where's Leicester?' the child asked.

'I think he's still asleep on his rug in the pantry,' Julie said. 'Don't play too hard, Kristen. He's getting awfully old, you know, but he loves you so much that he wears himself out when you're here.' The dog was getting so old, she thought with a pang, that he hadn't even raised a fuss last night when she and Greg had come in. That wasn't like Leicester. He had always been protective of his property. Was he getting deaf now, too, she wondered, as well as half-blind?

'May I take him for a walk?'

Julie shook her head. 'The men next door are working with big equipment,' she said. 'They might have trouble seeing you, and I don't want you and Leicester to be in danger.'

The child's face fell. Another one to chalk up to Greg's account, Julie reflected. 'You may take him out in the garden, though.'

Kristen thought it over and decided that it was better than nothing. 'All right.'

'But not outside the garden wall,' her mother ordered. She picked up a magazine and waved it like a fan. 'My gosh, it's stuffy in here, Julie.'

'This heatwave is just too much for the air-conditioning to keep up with.'

'It's got to break soon. It's been hot for two weeks.'

'I hope so. It'll be awful to have a holiday weekend with this kind of temperatures.'

'Speaking of holidays—why don't you come out to the house on Saturday? We'll lounge around by the pond, and cook hamburgers on the grill, and set off a few fireworks in the evening.'

'Who's coming?'

Sara grinned. 'Just a few friends. You are the most suspicious woman I've ever met, Julie.'

'Male friends? Unattached friends that I just might become attached to?'

'How did you guess?'

'Because we've played this scene before.'

'Nobody expects you to fall in love over the taco dip and be married before dessert, Julie. But if you'd just get to know a few men a little better—'

I have, Julie thought. Only two of them counted at

all; Keith wanted my pay cheques, and Greg wants my house. Oh, and they both are rather intrigued with my body as well, she reminded herself, but that definitely came second. As for my mind, that has been left out altogether. And I don't want any more of it.

If that was being an old maid, as Greg had scathingly accused her that morning—well, perhaps it was better to be a wise old maid than a wounded woman of the world.

'No, thanks,' she said.

'All right, stay in the city and swelter.' Sara was unoffended. 'I'll keep trying. Some day you'll decide that you want to associate with human beings of the opposite sex. Unless—is there something I should know about? Are you going to see Greg this weekend?' She leaned forwards, intrigued by this new possibility.

'Not if I can help it,' Julie said.

'I suppose that means he made a pass at you. For heaven's sake, Julie, aren't you ever normal? If that dreamboat made me an offer, I'd—'

'You wouldn't. You're a happily married woman.'

'I'd at least give it a lot of thought,' Sara concluded. 'Which is more than you appear to be doing.'

If you only knew, Julie thought.

Kristen burst into the room.

'Are you back already?' her mother asked.

'Leicester didn't want to go play in the garden. But Mommy, look what I found!'

Sara took the folded bit of paper without much interest.

'Is it a real dollar?' Kristen asked.

Sara unfolded it and sat up straight. 'Holy bananas, Kristen, where did you get this?'

'It was on the floor beside the front door. It doesn't look like a real dollar.'

'That's because it isn't one,' her mother said drily. 'Julie, I had no idea the shop was doing so well that you were flinging hundred-dollar bills around.'

Julie had forgotten all about Greg's money—the bill he had shoved at her the night before. 'Oh—' She saw the raging curiosity in Sara's eyes, and knew that trying to explain it would only make matters worse. 'It's supposed to be applied to a customer's account,' she said weakly.

Sara handed it over. 'And you treat it like this? Can I have a raise?'

Julie took the money gingerly, as if she expected it to scorch her hands. She sat twisting it between her fingers. I wish I'd remembered it when he was here this morning, she thought. I'd have rammed it down his throat. The sheer nerve of the man infuriated her. He had made giving her the money almost an obscene gesture. *'Remember that I'm first in line,'* indeed!

She shouldn't dwell on that, she told herself. It would only make her more angry. She'd mail the money back to him in an unmarked envelope. He'd know where it came from, and what the message was. It would serve him right if she tore it into bits first...

Or was there a better way? She had to get rid of this money somehow, without raising Sara's suspicions. She wasn't about to try to explain it to Sara, that was for sure. She shifted her weight on the stool, and her foot banged into the bottom drawer of the counter that held the cash register. She smiled, just a little, and reached for a pile of tissue paper and a box.

I'll teach Greg Roberts to throw his money around, she thought, with satisfaction.

Leicester did not want to go for a walk.

'I don't blame you,' Julie told him. 'I know that playing with Kristen wears you out. But you're an absolutely necessary prop. I know how hot it is out there, and I wouldn't go out myself if there was any other way—'

Leicester sighed and rolled over on his back. His tail thumped twice against the floor and then was still, as if he was trying to pretend he wasn't there at all.

Julie stooped over him and fastened the leash to his collar. Wearily, as if he knew he'd been out-manoeuvred, Leicester climbed to his feet.

Once outside, though, he made his usual turn east on Grand Avenue. 'Couldn't we have a short walk today, instead of doing the entire round?' Julie said. 'I don't want to kill either of us in the heat. I just want to—'

Leicester stopped and looked up at her, his plaintive eyes seeming to say that if something was worth doing at all, it was worth doing right. Julie subsided, shifted the weight of the silver-blue paper bag in her left hand, and loosened her grip on the leash so Leicester could have his head.

They made the usual circle, and Leicester obligingly stopped in front of the site of Greg's new office building. 'I didn't realise I'd gotten in the habit of standing here staring,' Julie said. She took a quick glance around. Greg's red sports car was still there, as she had hoped it would be. It was parked prominently and negligently near the construction driveway, and he was nowhere in sight. He must be inside, checking the work in progress on the lower floors. Good, she thought. That makes it a little easier.

She tightened her grip on Leicester's leash and on the paper bag, and started across the rough ground, chewed up by the passage of hundreds of trucks, towards the car.

A construction worker appeared. 'Ma'am!' he called. Julie ignored him. She was half-way to the car, and still there was no sign of Greg.

The worker broke into a run, each footfall kicking up a tiny spray of dust. 'Ma'am!' he shouted again. 'You can't come in here, ma'am!'

Julie didn't stop. 'Hello,' she said pleasantly as he fell into step beside her.

'This is a dangerous place, ma'am,' he said. 'You're trespassing, and I'll have to ask you to leave before you or the dog get hurt.'

'Oh, I'm not trespassing.' She waved the bag at him. 'I'm making a delivery.'

'But—but you can't do that,' he sputtered. 'I'll have to stop you. Now I don't want to get violent, but—'

'I'm only bringing Mr Roberts' package to him,' she explained patiently.

Greg's name, as she had expected, slowed the man down a bit. There was confusion in his eyes; he didn't want to get in trouble with the boss, that much was obvious.

Julie pressed her advantage. 'He bought this in my shop,' she explained. 'Exclusively Yours—it's a gift shop just about a block from here. He was in an awful hurry this morning and didn't want to wait for me to wrap it, but I know he's anxious to get this.'

'A gift shop?' the man said doubtfully. He pushed his hard hat back and scratched his head thoughtfully.

'Yes. Since I was planning to walk the dog anyway, I told him I'd drop the package off and save him the trouble of stopping by again.' And that, she congratulated herself, was as neat a piece of embroidering the truth as she was ever likely to do.

'Umm—well, I still can't let you go in,' he said. 'Tell you what, I'll leave the package in the guard shack. Mr Roberts will be sure to get it.'

'It isn't that I don't trust you,' she said politely. 'But it's fragile, and I don't think it should be left out where it might be dropped, or stepped on. It's a one-of-a-kind item, you see,' she added gently.

'All right,' the man capitulated. 'I'll put the darn thing in his car!'

Julie tried to look dubious, instead of triumphant. She handed the package over with a sigh. 'I suppose that's the best thing to do,' she said. 'If you'll put it on the front seat, so he'll be sure to see it right away...'

The workman looked down at the dainty package with its elaborate silver and white bow. 'You're sure he's expecting this?' he asked suspiciously.

'He certainly should be,' Julie said, with a perfectly straight face. She kept her composure until she was nearly a block from the site. Then she started to giggle hysterically as she imagined what Greg Roberts would do when he came back to his car and found an elegantly wrapped package awaiting him—a package that contained one very broken Bavarian lead crystal vase and thirteen crisp dollar bills, the change left from his hundred!

She snapped her fingers and swore. In her haste, she realised, she'd forgotten to charge him sales tax.

'I don't think you're going to like this,' Sara said the moment Julie came back in. 'But—'

'Please, let me enjoy my moment of triumph.' She unsnapped Leicester's leash and patted him. 'Thanks, buddy,' she said. 'You made all the difference in convincing him that I was for real.'

'I haven't the vaguest idea what you're talking about,' Sara said. 'I think the sun has curdled your blood. Walking the dog in this kind of weather—'

'I know. It's nice to be back in here.'

Sara looked at her in horror. 'Now I know you've cooked your brain. It is most certainly *not* nice in here. It is stuffy and hot, and it's going to get worse. What I'm trying to tell you, Julie, is that your air-conditioner has died. It is kaput. It has gone south for the winter. It has expired!'

'It can't do that. This is the hottest week of the year!'

'Well, it did.'

Julie sighed. 'One more bill. Well, I guess it can't be helped. Rosa put the thing in years ago. I'll call the repairman. We'll just have to take it easy till he fixes it, and—'

'That will be some time next week,' Sara interrupted. 'I already called him.'

Julie stopped in mid-step. 'He can't get here right away?'

'Not till Tuesday, to be precise. That is, if it doesn't rain in the meantime and slow him down,' Sara said helpfully. 'He can't work on electrical units in the rain, because he might fry himself.'

'Well, I'm not worried about rain. It hasn't rained for a month; why should it suddenly start now? But how am I supposed to run a business without air-conditioning for almost a week?'

'We're closed on Saturday and Sunday,' Sara volunteered. 'And tomorrow is a holiday, so I won't be coming to work—'

'You're very helpful,' Julie said.

'That just leaves Friday.'

'You forget that I have to live here, holiday or no holiday.'

'Oh, so that's what's bothering you,' Sara said on a note of ironic discovery. 'You're looking out for your own comfort.'

'Darn right I am. And Randie's health, as well.'

'Oh, I'd forgotten about Randie.'

'When you're over seventy, heat affects you differently. Randie would never admit to that, but it's downright dangerous for her.'

'You work up a good head of steam and call the repairman,' Sara suggested. 'And good luck. I already tried every nasty trick I know. By the way—'

'Sara, why is it that I get tense whenever you say that?'

Sara grinned. 'I've a bit of good news for you. You've got an invitation to tea this afternoon, and I'll bet it's cool there.'

'Where? With whom?'

Sara waved a bit of notepaper. 'Issued by telephone, with suitable apologies for short notice. I accepted for you, of course. You can't afford to turn this sort of thing down.'

'Sara!' Her voice was threatening.

'Annabel Hastings,' Sara said, lingering lovingly over each syllable. 'Lynne's grandma. And aren't you dying to go see what she wants from Exclusively Yours?'

The repairman was a wizened little guy, of an age somewhere between retirement and death, Julie thought. She leaned against the garden wall, feeling that, since he had made an exception and fitted this quick service call into his schedule, she didn't dare leave him alone. She had finally resorted to begging before he had given in.

'I'm awfully glad you could come by and take a look at it,' she said.

'Humpf.' He was head-first into the mechanism.

'I know Randie will appreciate it, too.'

'Yep.'

'You've known Randie a long time, haven't you?'

'Yep.'

Long moments of silence went by. She was beginning to feel like a wilted violet in the heat. 'Is it a big problem?' Julie asked nervously.

He looked up, finally. 'Needs cleaning.'

'Oh, is that all?' Relief bubbled in her voice.

'Not sure.' He looked up at the endloader across the driveway, piling rubble in the back of a dump truck. Two more trucks waited in line. 'They going to be doing that all summer?'

'I don't know; I suppose so. Is the dust what clogged it?' I'm going to end up suing Greg Roberts over this, she thought, wait and see if I don't!

'Didn't help it any. Fixin' it's easy enough.'

'That's good.'

'Yep. Take out this relic and put in a new one.'

'I understand,' Julie said. 'You said it would be *easy*. You didn't mean *inexpensive*.'

A grin cracked the weathered surface of the old man's face. 'That's right,' he said. 'But, considering everything—guess we'll just have to make do today. Wouldn't advise you do anything till they're done making a mess over there, anyway.'

Julie gritted her teeth as she looked across the vacant site. The mountain of rubble had been reduced to a pile, and a crew was unloading a mass of equipment from yet another truck. She didn't recognise any of it, but this must be what they were going to use to remove the concrete slab that formed the car park.

The repairman was playing a fine spray of water over the snakelike coils. 'Rosa put this thing in—must of been twenty years ago,' he said.

'Nevertheless,' Julie said, 'the state of my budget decrees that we'll use the old as long as it lasts.'

'Sure hope this does it,' he said, sounding less than convinced. 'When a piece of machinery gets this old, once it starts breaking down, it like to never is quite right again.'

'Thanks,' Julie said drily. 'That's just the kind of encouragement I needed to hear today.'

He was still working when she left the house to go to tea with Annabel Hastings. The bill is going to look like the national debt, she told herself with a shudder as she backed her dust-covered Edsel carefully out of the drive.

'Lynne's grandmother,' she muttered cynically as she walked into the quiet elegance of an upscale apartment house, smoothing her narrow white skirt and checking the bow at the neckline of her fuchsia blouse. 'You know darned well that you're not being summoned because of Lynne. Annabel Hastings is Greg's grandmother as well—' She congratulated herself for having read that newspaper article about the Hastings family; otherwise, that little revelation might have come as an unpleasant surprise. Now, the surprise might well be on the other foot…

She was startled when a grey-haired maid in a pale blue dress and white apron answered the door. No butler? Julie asked herself. Surely the dowager of the whole Hastings clan would surround herself with all the pomp and ceremony available to her. Or was it that she felt Julie unworthy of the display?

Well, my manners are as good as anybody's, Julie told herself. It's just that I don't choose to play the social games, so, if she's planning a charming afternoon of cat and mouse, she's going to be disappointed.

Or worse, she thought, if Annabel Hastings thinks that she can persuade me to sell Greg my house— It is really unfair of him, she thought, to use this sort of pressure.

Annabel Hastings was tiny, dainty, and charming, as far from the Amazon-sized steamroller that Julie had expected as it was possible to get. She jumped up from her chair like a teenager when the maid paused on the threshold to say, 'Miss Gordon, ma'am,' and came across the room with her hands outstretched. Beside this delicate lady, Julie felt like a gawky beanpole.

The blue eyes twinkled up at her. 'Do come and sit down, my dear. May I give you tea?' She didn't wait for an answer before beginning to manipulate the china pot.

That's Spode, Julie thought, or I'll eat it.

'I'm sorry about the late invitation,' the woman went on. 'I am delighted that you were able to come.'

'I couldn't stay away,' Julie said. If there was the faintest undercurrent of sarcasm in her voice, it was too vague to be noticed.

'Lemon? Sugar? Milk?'

'Lemon, please.' She took the cup. It was definitely Spode, she thought. And not the modern stuff, either.

'I wanted to give you my thanks for your help in making Lynne's wedding so special. The lace you provided for her gown was the most beautiful I've ever seen. I'm sorry I didn't have a chance to talk to you that night.' The dowager's eyes twinkled. 'You were very busy.'

Julie's eyes dropped, despite her best intentions. She swallowed hard and willed herself not to turn red at the mere reminder of what she must have appeared to be that night, with Greg at her side, making love to her with his eyes.

'I thought having tea together would be the next best thing,' Mrs Hastings went on. 'We should get to know each other, Miss Gordon.'

'Why?' Julie asked, baldly. 'Did you have the caterer and the florist to tea? I'm a merchant, just as they are.' She meant the words to sting.

Annabel Hastings smiled, and suddenly the room seemed to turn slightly pink around Julie. That's where Greg gets his charm, she thought. This is unfair, to have them ganging up on me.

She set the cup and saucer carefully aside and folded her hands in her lap. She looked like a prim schoolgirl, she supposed, but she didn't care; her fingers were clenched together to keep them from trembling. 'Why don't we put the cards on the table?' she said. 'I have many demands on my valuable time, and I'm sure you do as well. We both know that you haven't invited me here because of Lynne's wedding dress. I'm here because your grandson is trying to put me out of my house.'

Annabel Hastings paused in mid-motion, and then finished pouring her cup of tea. She set the pot carefully aside and said, 'That's quite true, Miss Gordon. I did invite you because of Greg. But—'

'I'm going to save us both a little trouble, Mrs Hastings. I am *not* going to sell my house to Greg, or to anyone else. Is that plain enough?'

'Have you finished?' Annabel Hastings said mildly.

'Oh, yes, quite.' Julie stood up.

'Then I wish you'd relax and enjoy your tea.' Julie

looked down at the woman in astonishment. There was nothing but mild concern in the lift of Annabel Hastings' eyebrows. 'You see, Julie, I haven't the vaguest desire to talk you into selling your house.'

'You don't?'

'No, my dear. Quite the opposite, in fact.' She smiled with what looked like real amusement. 'I've been longing to meet you, Juliet Gordon—the girl whom my grandson's money cannot buy.'

CHAPTER SIX

JULIE sat down abruptly on the brocade love-seat, feeling as if all the bones in her body had just dissolved.

Annabel Hastings smiled brilliantly. 'Would you like a sandwich, dear? The cucumber ones are a particular favourite of mine.'

Julie shook her head absently. 'But I thought you'd be upset,' she said. 'He's put a lot of money into this project, and without my house—which I assure you he won't get—he's going to lose it all.'

'Oh, I don't think you need concern yourself about that. Gregory is quite able to afford this hobby of his, you know.'

A hobby, Julie thought hollowly. Constructing office buildings and condominium towers is what Annabel Hastings thinks of as a hobby? I am, without a doubt, in over my head, she told herself.

'You sound,' she said carefully, 'as if you'd like to see him lose the whole works.'

'Oh, I don't think I'd go quite so far as that,' Annabel said. 'But I think it's healthy now and then for the irresistible force to run into the immovable object. You see, Greg has very seldom been told that he couldn't have something. He was an only child, and his mother, my daughter, Louise, was not, perhaps, the wisest of parents.' A brief shadow crossed her face.

I really don't care, Julie thought. He could have had

the most miserable childhood in the world, and it wouldn't change the way I feel about him. He's a selfish, stubborn brute who thinks of nothing but himself, and if his grandmother believes that telling me a sob story is going to soften me up and make me feel sorry for the poor boy, she just doesn't know me very well!

'Louise was not happy in her marriage,' Annabel went on after a brief pause, 'and she turned on her son all the attention and devotion that rightly belonged to her husband. It was unfortunate for all of them, but especially for Greg. He was fast growing up to be a terror, when—'

'He still is a terror,' Julie murmured.

Annabel smiled at the interruption, but shook her head. 'If it hadn't been for his essentially sweet nature, Louise would have completely ruined him.'

Julie held her peace and nibbled at a cucumber sandwich. His sweet nature, my foot! she thought. It was obvious to her that his grandmother was prejudiced.

'When Greg was twelve, his father died, and within a few months Louise remarried. Greg was not fond of his stepfather, and he didn't like the idea of suddenly being pushed aside. He developed quite a knack, as children of broken homes will, of getting his own way.'

'Which he has since polished into a fine art,' Julie said smoothly.

'Now, really! He's not some kind of vulture, Juliet. He may bluster and threaten, but he can't do a single thing about that house of yours unless you change your mind.'

'No?' Julie said doubtfully. 'Well, you may be right—but let me tell you, it isn't very comfortable being in my shoes. I keep thinking that, if I could just turn around fast enough, I could see him plotting against me, and then I'd know what he was going to do next.'

'That would be a handy talent, wouldn't it? I don't believe I'd fret about the house, my dear. It's perfectly safe.'

'I beg your pardon for my frankness,' Julie said, 'but I fret about it a great deal. I haven't any idea what to do about him, you see. He just won't take no for an answer—'

'I've found,' Annabel said calmly, 'that the most complicated problems often call for the simplest of solutions.'

That was easy enough for her to say, Julie thought. Presumably, Greg's grandmother had never been on the wrong end of one of his schemes. 'I appreciate the advice,' she said, 'but I think I'll try to cultivate eyes in the back of my head.'

'Not a bad idea,' said a voice behind her. 'Tell me, when do you plan to start?'

Julie jumped and spilled her tea. She looked accusingly across the small table at Annabel, who said, mildly, 'Good afternoon, Gregory. Would you like tea?'

'No, thank you.' Greg crossed the room to a built-in cabinet, and opened a door to reveal a row of gleaming bottles. 'I think it will take something stronger. What is *she* doing here?' He gestured to Julie with a bottle of Scotch.

'Visiting me,' his grandmother said, distinctly. 'You can see, of course, Juliet, that I did not plan this. If I had, I would have made certain that my grandson would remember his manners.'

Julie couldn't help smiling a little. 'That's difficult enough for him at the best of times,' she said.

'I quite agree. Gregory has these unfortunate lapses now and then.'

'If you're trying to get me to leave, Grandmother…'

'Of course not, dear. I'm quite delighted that you stopped in. I was just trying to get you to behave in a civilised manner.'

'I was simply bowled over at the charm of your lovely visitor,' he drawled. He sat down beside Julie on the love-seat, quite a bit closer than she thought was necessary, and leaned back, his legs stretched out, his glass held loosely in one hand. The other arm lay carelessly across the back of the love-seat.

Surely he wasn't going to make a scene in his grandmother's home? Julie thought with a twinge of panic. He hadn't hesitated at Lynne's wedding, in front of the whole family. But surely this was different?

'Thank you,' he said, looking down at her with a glint in his brown eyes, 'for the gift you so thoughtfully brought me today.'

She wanted to heave a giant sigh of relief. He was exacting punishment, she thought, that was all. He was going to play a little cat and mouse game of his own, under his grandmother's nose, knowing that it would make Julie squirm. But he wouldn't carry it to embarrassing lengths. After all, he'd be embarrassed by it, too.

'It wasn't a gift,' she said quickly. 'It's yours—you paid for it.'

He shook his head. 'Oh, no,' he said. 'That wasn't what I ordered at all.'

'I'm afraid that's the closest you're going to come,' she said, forcing herself to smile sweetly up at him.

'Would you care to place a little wager on that?' His arm slipped a bit closer to her, until she could feel the sleeve of his jacket brushing her hair. 'You do have a reputation, Juliet, for providing what the customer wants, no matter how—' He paused, then added thoughtfully, 'No matter how exotic.'

She knew she shouldn't look at him, and yet she didn't have the will-power to deny the husky demand in that low voice. Her dark green eyes lifted to meet his, and the glow she saw there—a strange combination of anger and desire, of mischief and of certainty—seemed to drag the life's breath out of her and leave her gasping for sustenance. She licked her lips nervously, and saw his eyes focus on the tip of her tongue. His body tensed, and she knew as clearly as if he had shouted it what he wanted to do, what he would have done had Annabel Hastings not been pouring tea across the table, supremely unaware of what was going on between her two guests.

If they had been alone, Julie thought, he would have crushed her mouth under his, taking, demanding, plundering, caressing, until every restraint was forgotten, until her body exploded in a sheet of flame and she begged him to make love to her. Begged him, as she so nearly had last night.

'I don't think it would be difficult at all, for you to get me what I want,' he murmured, and the words themselves were a husky seduction, promising her the earth and the skies and all the beauty two human bodies could share. His fingers brushed the nape of her neck, under the curtain of hair. It was a more intimate touch than any other caress could have been.

'Would you like another cup of tea, Juliet?' Annabel asked.

Julie pulled the scattered bits of her poise together. 'No, thank you, Mrs Hastings,' she said. 'I—I really must be going.'

'Then you must come again soon,' Annabel said. 'Next time, we'll have Lynne join us, if you like.'

Julie stood up quickly. Her forgotten linen napkin fluttered from her lap to the floor; she bent quickly to retrieve it, and nearly bumped her head against Greg's. He took the napkin from her, brushing his fingers along the back of her hand and making the simple gesture into an object lesson. Just like this, he seemed to be saying, I could make you respond to me, if I chose.

'Surely you aren't going yet, Gregory.' Annabel's words were more a statement than a request. 'There are some things I need to discuss with you.'

There was a tiny, breathless pause, and then Greg said smoothly, 'Of course not, Grandmother. I'll just walk Julie to her car, and I'll be back.'

'Please don't come with me,' Julie breathed.

'Why not? I only want to say goodbye.'

'I'd rather—' She stopped, no longer sure of what she meant. 'She doesn't want you to.'

He didn't answer. 'I'm going out of town tomorrow.'

'Why are you telling me that? Do you think I care?' Julie retorted, with the last flash of spirit that she could muster.

His crooked, little-boy smile flashed. 'I'm telling you,' he said, 'just in case you miss me. I wouldn't want you to think I've given up my place in line.'

She didn't go home right away. Sara would have closed the shop and left by now, but Randie would be there, full of questions. And just now, Julie knew, she couldn't face Randie's gentle, innocent enquiries. So she drove up and down the winding streets of Des Moines' residential neighbourhoods, and through the parks, while she struggled to deal with her confusion.

She was confused about herself, about the way she felt any time she was near Greg Roberts. She was confused about him; just this morning, when he had returned her jacket to the house, he had acted as though he never wanted to see her again. But this afternoon, he had been blatantly seducing her in his grandmother's living-room. Just what was going on in Greg's mind? she wondered. And what was the matter with her that she had sat still and let him get away with it? If he had tried that trick anywhere else, she'd have been in bed with him by now.

Perhaps that, she told herself bleakly, is why he chose that place, and that time. Because he knew that the fun couldn't get out of hand.

He could have followed me, she reminded herself. He started to, and then Annabel stopped him. It had been a lucky rescue, she told herself.

Just what did Greg want, anyway? What kind of stakes was he playing for? The house? Or was it more than that?

Thank heaven, she thought, that Annabel Hastings had remained sublimely unaware of what was occurring on her love-seat. If she had realised what Greg was up to...

But of course she had known, Julie realised. The woman was not blind.

'She had to know,' she said breathlessly, and her face flamed with colour. 'She was at the wedding, and saw how he behaved there. She was sitting across from us today. She knew what he was thinking.'

And, knowing, she had quietly stopped Greg from leaving her apartment.

'She didn't want him to come with me,' Julie told herself. Somehow, she had failed Annabel Hastings' test.

That's dumb, she told herself. Perhaps I passed it, instead, and convinced the woman that I'm too good to be wasted on Greg Roberts.

She didn't believe it, of course. Annabel Hastings might admit Greg's faults, but it was obvious that she thought the world of him. And as for Greg...

'Somehow,' Julie murmured, 'I get the feeling that her opinion is the only one in the world he thinks much of.'

So, Annabel had crooked a finger, and Greg had stayed.

'And I'm glad,' Julie told herself stoutly. It could only have been trouble for her otherwise. Perhaps this would be the end of it. Perhaps Annabel had kept him there to talk some sense into him, and Julie would never have to see him again.

It left her feeling quite alone, and exquisitely miserable, and with an unaccountable desire to cry.

The repairman's work had been in vain. By Thursday morning, the air-conditioning system had broken down again. By the time Julie discovered it, the house was growing steadily hotter and the repairman had apparently left town. His answering service promised blithely that he would call her the following week. Julie gave up on him and gritted her teeth, determined to make the best of it.

Thursday was bearable; with the holiday, the workmen were gone, and the dust had settled over the vacant site. The open windows let in a fitful breeze. When Julie took Leicester for his walk that evening, she inspected the work that had been done so far. A good portion of the cement had been sawed into neat four-foot-square blocks; Julie assumed that, after the holiday weekend, the endloader would pick up each section and deposit it in a truck to be hauled away.

'It's a waste of natural resources, Leicester,' she told the dog, who looked near-sightedly at the concrete and then sneezed. 'Dust,' Julie said. 'You don't understand it, do you? Hold on to your patience; they'll be done in a few days.' She wasn't quite sure if she was talking to the dog, or to herself.

Friday dawned like a blast furnace. The sky had that

particular brassy tinge that marked the hottest of summer days in Iowa, and the pavement seemed to be melting before nine in the morning. The humid heat poured into the house and soaked into the bricks, the glass, the plaster. The woodwork felt sticky, and a careless hand against the century-old varnish left fingerprints. By mid-afternoon, the three adults in the house were all short-tempered, but too worn out even to snap at one another. The only one who escaped was Kristen, who had spent the day splashing in a plastic wading pool in the backyard.

'Oh, for the energy of youth,' her mother sighed.

'And for a figure that looks that good in a swimsuit,' Julie added. 'I wish I could run the shop dressed that way.'

'I know one customer who would stop in as soon as he heard about it,' Sara gibed.

Julie didn't turn a hair; she was getting used to Sara's hints about Greg, and she didn't want to encourage the woman by reacting. If Sara found out that he'd made a point of telling Julie he was going out of town, she'd make a production of it.

Randie was the one who was most obviously miserable. She sat in her rocking-chair in the corner of the kitchen, her face flushed with heat, and fanned herself listlessly.

Julie went to the kitchen for the tenth time herself to make yet another pitcher of iced tea, and paused in the middle of the floor with her hands on her hips. 'Look, Randie,' she announced, 'I've had it with arguing. You're going to stay someplace where you can be cool.'

'It's just as hot for you.'

'Companionship is not the point. I have a business to run, and things that keep me from leaving.' She sighed.

'It looks as if it may storm this afternoon, and break the heat.'

'It will help for a while, but it will be just as hot and sticky by tomorrow. Randie, we've got a whole weekend of this to get through.'

'Then why don't you come away, too?'

Julie bit her lip, and then said, honestly, 'Because I'm damned if he's going to drive me away from my house.'

'Gregory did not break the air-conditioning,' Randie pointed out.

'No? Well, he'd certainly take advantage of it, if he could see an opportunity.'

Randie sighed. 'Won't you at least think hard about what we're going to do, Juliet?'

'I know what *you're* going to do. You're going to run along upstairs and put some clothes in a bag, and Sara's going to take you out to her house on the lake before you collapse of heat exhaustion. Come on, I'll help you.'

For a moment, it seemed as if Randie hadn't heard. Then she slowly pulled herself out of the chair. 'I can drive,' she said, but she sounded doubtful.

'You're not going to.' Julie breathed a thankful sigh when Randie showed no further inclination to argue. She wasn't fit to drive today. Besides, Julie thought, if Randie had her car she could change her mind and come home any time, whether it was cool or not, and then they'd have the battle to fight all over again.

'What are we going to do?' the woman asked as Julie was packing her suitcase. 'I know you didn't sleep last night, Juliet. I heard you pacing along the upstairs hall. What happens if the thing can't be fixed? We can't afford to put in new air-conditioning right now.'

'There's plenty of time to worry about that if it happens, and it isn't going to happen,' Julie said, with a lot more certainty that she felt.

'But if we sell the house, we'll have plenty to keep us in comfort. You could have another little shop, and I could have—' She stopped. 'I shouldn't talk about it. I'm not feeling very well today, I'm afraid.'

Julie closed the case and pulled the chair out from Randie's dressing-table. 'What is it, exactly, that you want, Randie?' she asked gently.

'Do you know, my dear,' Randie said softly, 'I think that's the first time you've ever asked me.'

Julie tried not to feel defensive. 'I always assumed that you loved it here. You certainly did a good imitation of it. One of the first things I remember is you cleaning the house—standing on a ladder in the drawing-room and polishing the crystal drops on the chandelier till every one shone like a star.'

'I always tried to help Rosa however I could,' Randie said. 'She was providing me with a home, and I didn't want to be in her way.'

Julie folded her hands along the back of her chair and leaned her chin on them. 'But you felt like a charity case?'

Randie nodded. 'Yes, I suppose I did.' She sighed unhappily. 'I always wanted just a little place of my own. A tiny apartment would have been enough. The important thing was that it be mine. I had just a little money that I'd inherited from my father, and I had made up my mind. I'd even found my own place, and I braced myself to tell Rosa that I was going to move. She wouldn't have taken it very well, I'm afraid. It wasn't long after her husband died.'

Her voice trailed off, and after a long pause, Julie said, 'But you didn't do it?'

'No.'

'Why not?'

Randie seemed to pull herself together. Her vagueness vanished. 'Circumstances intervened. I was needed here. There's no need to discuss it further, Julie.' Randie's mouth was tight. 'I shouldn't have mentioned it, but I wanted you to understand that I have no great attachment to this house, and so if you're hanging on to it out of some mistaken desire not to rob me of my home—'

Julie wasn't listening. 'Not long after Uncle Sid died,' she mused, and looked up with dawning horror in her eyes. 'But that's when my father brought me back here, and dumped me off for you and Rosa to raise—'

'"Dumped you off" is scarcely the way I would have put it,' Randie said primly.

'But that's what it was, wasn't it?'

Randie sighed. 'I wish you hadn't made the connection, my dear. Someone had to take the responsibility. You were so very small. Rosa couldn't handle you alone. Neither could I. So—'

'So Randie the saint, without a word, gave up her own dream and took on a child to raise. Oh, darling, I *am* sorry!' She gave her aunt a quick, impulsive hug.

'I shouldn't have upset you with it,' Randie said. 'I don't mean to make myself out to be a martyr, my dear. You were a beautiful little girl, and I wanted to take care of you.'

But now what? Julie thought. What happens when Randie's wishes, and mine, are so completely opposite that there isn't even a way to compromise?

I'll think about it later, when my head is clear, she decided, and picked up Randie's suitcase. 'Let's get you off to the lake, and we'll talk about it some other time,' she promised.

'You must do as you wish, Juliet.' Randie had obviously seen the perplexed frown on her face. 'It's your wishes that are important now.'

Because Randie doesn't think she's going to be around that long, Julie finished the thought. And she ought to have what she wants, if it's possible, even if it's only for a little time.

She looked around the big, high-ceilinged bedroom, with its Victorian print wallpaper and heavy wood mouldings and the fluted glass chandelier that had once been lit by gas. To her, it was one of the most beautiful things on earth. But if, to Randie, it was some sort of prison...

What am I to do? Julie thought. She gave up everything for me, when I was only a child and needed her. And now, she's something like a child, and she needs me.

Sara put Randie's luggage into her car and called for Kristen. The little girl dragged her feet as she came unwillingly to the garden gate. She was dripping from the pool. 'Do I have to come, Mommy?' she pleaded. 'I want to stay in the water.'

Sara rolled her eyes. 'I'm raising a crazy child,' she said. 'She wants to stick around this giant barbecue pit?'

'You don't want her dripping all over the car,' Julie said mildly.

'There is that. If you really don't mind keeping her—'

'What I want,' Julie said, 'is to get Randie out of this heat before she changes her mind and refuses to go.'

'Good point. I'll call her father and have him pick Kristen up after work.' She grinned. 'That way she can drip all over *his* car.'

After they were gone, Julie hosed the slimy grey mud off Kristen's feet and put her back in the pool. The chalky dust must be pure cement, she thought; when water touched it, it turned into a sludgy puddle. Her garden was going to be a wreck all summer. Already the flowers looked droopy and sad, as if they'd been beaten. If they survived at all, it would be a wonder.

She thought fleetingly about putting a 'closed' sign on the door and joining Kristen in the pool, but she went back inside. Business was usually good on Friday afternoons, and heaven knew she couldn't afford to turn a customer away just now.

Besides, she thought as the cement saws started up again next door, if she stayed outdoors, that high-pitched whine would drive her swiftly into a mad-house. At least inside, even with the windows open, it wasn't quite so loud. And, as if the cement saws weren't bad enough, today they had brought in a couple of jackhammers and were pounding the squares of concrete into fist-size chunks to be hauled away. It seemed to her to be needless work. Another day of this, she thought, and I may just start to scream right along with the saws.

She was standing on a dining-room chair and cleaning the talcum-powdery dust off the shelves of antique crystal when the bell warned her that someone had come in. She set a crystal bowl back carefully in its place, just in case her visitor was Greg, and climbed down, smoothing her skirt as she went into the drawing-room.

It was Mrs Baxter, the one who had bought the expensive goblet a few days before. 'Marian was thrilled to get it,' she said. 'I told her I'd ask you to let her know if you get others. She's been collecting that pattern for years, you know.'

'I'd be happy to. Is there something else I could show you today?'

'Well, something for my niece's birthday, I think.'

'Something personalised? I have some pretty stationery, and we can monogram it for her.'

'Teenagers can't seem to write at all these days.

Goodness knows, they never even bother with thank-you letters!'

'That's true enough, I'm afraid. How about a piece of art, or a special book?'

Mrs Baxter looked surprised. 'You have books, too?'

'Well, it's not a bookstore in the established sense. But I pick up some unusual editions now and then.' Julie led the way back to the library, where high windows stood open to the heat. The books were protected by leaded-glass doors over every bookcase, but she wondered how long that could keep the humidity from damaging the fragile leather bindings.

Mrs Baxter waved her hand. 'A little warm in here, isn't it?'

'Yes, I'm afraid it is. We've had a mechanical breakdown.'

'Well, I don't suppose there's much point in fixing it, is there?' The woman's smile was a sly smirk.

'I don't quite understand what you mean,' Julie said.

'Is it a secret, then?' Mrs Baxter put a hand on Julie's arm. 'I shan't breathe a word. But shall we say, just between us, that I know someone who would love to have these doors? So when you're ready, just call me, and I'll—'

'Ready for what?' Julie said icily.

'Oh, I assumed that you kept salvage rights. I mean, everybody knows that Greg isn't interested in the house itself, just the—'

Julie saw red. So he was letting it be known that the bargain had been struck, was he? 'You seem to be implying that I'm going to sell this house a bit at a time and let Greg Roberts tear down whatever is left.'

Mrs Baxter looked astounded. 'Do you mean, you aren't?'

'Absolutely not,' Julie snapped. She would have liked to say a great deal more, but she retained enough common sense to know that, whatever Mrs Baxter knew, she told.

'But I was sure—' Mrs Baxter paused and then shook her head. 'Marian said she asked him about it, and he told her everything was going as planned. You really aren't going to sell it, then?'

Julie swallowed her anger with an effort, and said, 'If your niece happens to like historical romances, here's an unusual edition of Jane Austen.'

Mrs Baxter eventually bought a blown glass swan, made by a local craftsman who brought his work to Julie on consignment. 'I suppose she'll use it as an ashtray,' she commented as she paid the bill. 'I haven't the least idea what this generation is coming to.'

'I suppose that's been said about every group of young people through history.' Julie wrote up the receipt.

'Well, I must say I'm glad to know you'll still be here,' Mrs Baxter said, tucking the package under her arm. 'We wouldn't know what to do without you. And don't worry. I won't breathe a word to anyone.'

At least, Julie thought, not to anyone beyond her hairdresser, her manicurist, her housekeeper, and her hundred or so best friends!

With her customer safely gone, Julie let herself feel the anger that had been bubbling deep inside since Mrs

Baxter's ill-chosen remark. So Greg was so certain of himself that he wasn't even troubling to deny comment, she thought. He was going around telling people that everything was going as planned!

And perhaps it was, she told herself. Perhaps he had planned this job to be slow and noisy and absolutely impossible to live with. Perhaps he was just waiting for her to snap, and give up, rather than have to listen to a cement saw and a jackhammer for one more hour.

Fury welled up inside her. It was about time, she thought, that someone told Greg Roberts no and made it stick. He didn't seem to listen to ordinary means.

The promised storm struck at mid-afternoon. Kristen came tearing in from the garden, leaving muddy footprints through the kitchen and down the glossy parquet floor of the hall. 'The thunder scared me,' she announced breathlessly when she caught up with Julie, who was frantically closing windows against the torrential rain.

'I can see why,' Julie said, as a particularly close lightning bolt made the earth sizzle. 'Look, even Leicester is scared of the storm.' The old dog had crept under a claw-footed table in the front hallway. 'Let's get you cleaned up and dry so you'll be ready when your daddy comes.'

'I want to stay with you. You always do such fun things.'

'That's a lovely thought. Later this summer you can stay a whole weekend with me, and we'll do lots of special things.' She washed the splashes of cement mud off Kristen's sturdy legs and wrapped her legs in a big fluffy towel. 'If the rain stops soon, we'll give you a real bath,' she promised. 'I don't want to put you in water as long as the storm is going on.'

Rain poured from the leaden sky and pounded against the slate roof—more water, it seemed, than had fallen all spring. Julie and Kristen sat curled up together on the front porch, enjoying nature's fireworks display and basking in the cool breeze.

The workers next door had taken shelter in their trucks when the rain began. They looked cramped and miserable there, but Julie hardened her heart. If they wanted shelter, she thought, they should tell their boss to provide it. Besides, by the time they could have crossed the lot and her driveway to shelter on the porch, they'd have been soaked through. A storm this intense couldn't last long, she told herself.

It didn't, but Kristen had fallen asleep by the time the rain stopped, and so Julie sat there on the porch swing with the child's head in her lap, rocking gently back and forth, enjoying the silence after the storm and watching the rainbow that briefly appeared over downtown Des Moines. She tried to wake Kristen to admire the colours, but the child muttered sleepily and buried her face in the yellow cotton of Julie's skirt.

The men went back to work. So much for peace and quiet, Julie thought as she heard the endloader start up. But surely it wasn't safe to run some of that equipment on wet ground? Perhaps, she thought, if she was lucky, they'd take off early.

She was half-asleep herself, sitting there in the comfortable swing, when the crash came. The house seemed to shudder around her, and she slid Kristen off her lap and was down the steps and around to the side of the house before the child could do more than murmur.

The driveway was kerb-deep in grey-brown water, the run-off from the car park. That was bad enough, Julie thought; she'd never had water run on to her property like that before, no matter how bad a storm was. But it paled when she saw what had happened at the back of the parking area. The operator of the end-loader had been moving it, and had got too close to the boundary of the parking area. He had lost traction in a puddle of the slimy concrete mud and slid out of control, smashing into the back of her car. Her precious vintage Edsel!

Julie started to run. She was nearly ankle-deep in water, and with every step the mud seemed to drag her down. She was almost to the car when the boss of the demolition crew caught up with her.

'I'm awful sorry,' he said. 'Didn't realise that stuff would be so slick.'

'Then you should have,' she spat. 'It's your business to know things like that!'

'Now, no need to get upset,' he said. 'Mr Roberts will make the damage good, I'm sure.'

'Mr Roberts,' she said, with biting sarcasm, 'has done all the damage to my property that he is going to do. You can inform him for me that I plan to take action!'

'I understand you being angry,' the foreman said reasonably, 'but a lawyer would cost you a lot more than the car's worth.'

'I didn't say I was going to hire a lawyer.' Her voice was even, almost pleasant. 'I'm going to take my case to an even higher court. Let's see what the citizens of Des Moines think about this.'

She turned on her heel. Her shoe caught in a crack in the driveway which had been concealed by the rushing water, and she went down with a splash in the mud.

She sat there for a moment, with water soaking every fibre of her clothes, and grimaced. 'That does it,' she said. Then she spat a loose lock of hair out of her mouth, and looked up at the foreman. 'Would you give me a hand up?' she asked politely.

He did. 'You'll feel better with some clean clothes on,' he said, hopefully.

'I know something that will make me feel much better than that,' she said. 'You might want to call Mr Roberts and explain what happened. And tell him from me that the picket lines are going up tonight!'

CHAPTER SEVEN

KRISTEN tiptoed down the hallway and stopped within three feet of where Julie was kneeling. She stood on one bare foot, twisting her toes restlessly, and put her thumb in her mouth while she watched Julie. Finally she removed the thumb and observed, 'You're making puddles on your pretty wood floor.'

'I am above being concerned about such mundane things as muddy floors,' Julie said grandly. She sat back on her heels and inspected her project, then reached for a purple marking pen.

'What are you doing?'

'Kristen, I am about to give you a lesson in politics. I am going to illustrate the principle of democracy that says everyone is entitled to free speech, by going out on the street and speaking very freely.'

Kristen looked puzzled. 'Can I go?'

'Can you go?' Julie smiled at the child. 'Of course you can. I couldn't do without you. In fact, I'm making your sign right now.'

Kristen grinned shyly. 'What does it say?'

'Greg Roberts is a homewrecker,' Julie said under her breath. She coloured in the last letter. 'Here you go, midget.' She picked up Leicester's leash and her own sign, a neon-coloured marvel that shouted, *He destroyed my car—is my house next?* 'Let's go, partner.'

'Leicester doesn't have a sign.'

'He's only going along for atmosphere.'

Kristen looked a little doubtful. Julie didn't argue; she simply wrapped Leicester's leash around her wrist and took Kristen by the hand.

It was the beginning of rush-hour on Friday afternoon, the time when Grand Avenue carried its heaviest traffic of home-bound workers. 'Perfect timing,' Julie congratulated herself. 'Stay on the pavement, Kristen.'

'But don't you want Greg to read your sign?'

'I think he'll hear all about it soon enough. And I don't want to be arrested for trespassing. We'll just walk back and forth out here and wait for him to come.'

The construction workers spotted them immediately, and the foreman came rushing out to the pavement. 'You can't do this, lady,' he said.

Julie looked down her nose at him. 'Why don't you call your boss,' she suggested politely, 'and ask him if it's legal for a citizen to walk up and down a city pavement carrying a sign? Use my phone, if you like.' She turned her back on him and sauntered up the path, making sure that her sign was readable from the street.

Kristen gave a little skip. 'This is fun, Julie. Wait till I tell Mommy what I did today.'

Julie felt the first twinge of doubt. Then she smothered it. After all, she couldn't leave the child alone in the house, could she?

With the cement saws, the jackhammers, and the endloader quiet, the only sounds were the buzz of traffic on the wide avenue and the gurgle of rain-water cascading down to the storm sewers. Julie and Kristen and Leicester walked slowly up and down. They had made the circuit only a half dozen times when a police car pulled up into the driveway. There was no siren, but the red lights atop the car were flashing wildly.

Kristen stopped and watched in fascination as the uniformed police officer got out. 'Shall I put up my hands?' she asked.

'No, dear. He isn't going to arrest us, because we haven't done anything wrong. Good afternoon, officer,' she said with a smile.

He read her sign, and his eyebrows went up. 'Who's in charge here?' he asked.

The foreman scurried up. 'This kooky dame is getting in the way of my crew's work,' he said.

Julie noted the description with interest. She'd gone from *ma'am* to *lady* to *kooky dame* in a matter of minutes.

'Are you Roberts?' the officer asked, gesturing towards Kristen's sign.

'No, sir. That's my boss.'

'Why is his name on the sign?' the officer asked Julie.

'Because he's the boss,' she said. 'And I'm holding him responsible for the damage to my car.'

The policeman looked a little dizzy. 'What car? They told me this was a civil disturbance. Nobody said anything about an accident.'

'There is some debate,' Julie said pointedly, 'as to whether it was accidental. The car is in my driveway—there. It's the one the endloader slid into.'

The foreman groaned. 'I've already told her the boss

would make it good. It's an old car, and it's only a scratch.'

Julie glared at him. 'It's an antique car,' she corrected, 'and it is a dent!'

The policeman sighed. 'If you'll both come sit in the squad car,' he said, 'we'll fill out an accident report, and—'

'Can't we do it here?' Julie asked. 'I would prefer to continue picketing.'

'There isn't enough damage to need a damned report,' the foreman said. 'I told you, it's only a scratch. What I want is to get this dame, her kid, and her dog off the property so I can get my men back to work.'

'I'm not on the property,' Julie pointed out. 'I am on a public pavement. I have every right to be here.'

The officer looked at the sky, pushed his cap back, and rubbed his nose. 'Why do they always send me on the wacky ones?' he asked no one in particular. He turned to the foreman. 'Have you told your boss about this?'

'No. I thought you'd take care of the problem,' he said belligerently. 'Isn't that what the cops are for?'

'Well, let's notify him, shall we?' The officer pulled the walkie-talkie off his belt and called the police dispatcher. 'What's his name?'

The foreman looked sulky. Julie said, clearly, 'Gregory Roberts. Roberts Development Corporation.'

The cop looked at her suspiciously, and repeated the information. 'Find the guy,' he ordered, 'and tell him he's got a disturbance going on at his construction site on Grand Avenue.' He put the radio back on his belt.

'Now, we'll just wait for him to show up,' he said. 'If you'd like to sit in the car, ma'am—'

'No, thank you,' Julie said. 'I'll just stroll up and down out here.'

'Don't block the trucks,' he warned.

She smiled. 'I won't,' she said. 'I wouldn't dream of interfering with the normal course of business. But you might want to move the squad car out of their way.'

A dump truck screeched to a halt on Grand Avenue and the driver leaned out of the window to study Julie's sign. The cop backed his car out on to the avenue and left it blocking a lane of traffic, the red lights still flashing. He and the foreman walked back towards Julie's car, which sat forlornly at the far end of the driveway, with the endloader still resting against the rear fender.

With a gnashing of gears, the dump truck turned slowly into the drive, bounced over the rough cement, and pulled up to the loading area. The driver got out and stood beside the wheel, staring at Julie's sign. 'I'm a union man myself,' he said. 'But I'm damned if I ever saw a picket line like this one.'

The foreman and the officer came back to the street. 'What do you mean, you can't haul her off?' the foreman was saying. It sounded like a strangled scream.

'If you don't want her here, see a judge. He might give you an injunction.'

'She's a blasted nuisance!'

The policeman shrugged. 'It's a public sidewalk. She's got a right to free speech.'

'See, Kristen?' Julie said. 'I told you so.'

'The worst I can charge her with is exaggeration,' the cop went on, and turned to Julie. 'The car is not destroyed, ma'am.'

'Tell me, officer, if that was your 1958 Edsel, and if someone drove an endloader into the corner of it, what would you do?'

He grinned. 'I see your point. I'd talk to the man in charge, I suppose.'

'That's what I'm going to do,' she said sweetly. 'Very soon now.'

A small red sports car wheeled around the parked police car and into the end of Julie's drive, and screeched to a halt. Greg got out. He crossed the pavement slowly, assessing the scene, and as he came up to the small group he was smiling. But the humour did not reach his eyes.

'I see you've been having a bad day, Julie,' he murmured. 'Would someone like to tell me about it?'

'I thought perhaps you could sort this out, sir,' the officer said. 'I don't seem to be doing too well.'

'Considering the material you have to work with,' Greg said, with a sidelong glance at Julie, 'I'm not surprised. Julie, did you have to drag the kid in on it, too? You do realise that sign she's carrying is slanderous, don't you?'

'Isn't it libel when it's written down? Really, Greg, how heartless it would be of you to have Kristen hauled into court for libelling you.'

'Kristen can't pronounce *homewrecker*,' he said tartly, 'much less spell it. Why don't you put the signs away? We'll go discuss this like civilised people over a steak somewhere.' His eyes focused suddenly on Julie's sign, which had been turned away. 'What do you mean, I destroyed your car?'

Julie pointed towards the back of the driveway.

Greg's face turned pasty white under his tan. 'The Edsel?'

'It's not destroyed, exactly,' the cop said.

'It's only a damned scratch!' the foreman yelled. He pulled off his hard hat in frustration and threw it on the ground. It bounced.

'Then you'll take responsibility, Mr Roberts?' the police officer questioned.

'I suppose I have no choice,' Greg said. 'It's obviously my equipment that did the damage.'

'Thank you,' Julie said. 'I half expected that you'd accuse me of backing into your endloader and scratching it.'

'Then that settles it,' the officer said with a relieved sigh. 'Let's make out the report, and—'

Greg's arms went around Julie and pulled her tightly against him. She panicked and fought him, but her hands were occupied with the sign and the dog. 'Let me go, you ape—' she started to say.

A speeding car struck a sheet of muddy water that had pooled near the kerb, and the resulting splash caught Julie full across the face. She started to splutter.

'I did try to pull you away,' Greg said smoothly, flicking a few drops of water from his trousers.

She opened and shut her mouth several times, but no sound would come out.

A small car pulled up to the kerb. 'Would someone mind explaining what's going on?' Sara asked plaintively, leaning out the window. 'I leave my daughter for a while, and I come back to find her in custody.'

'It isn't even the dame's own kid?' the foreman muttered. 'And I thought she was trying to make out that the boss was the kid's dad!' He caught a fuming look from Greg, and subsided.

Kristen blithely handed her sign to Greg and skipped across the pavement to hop into the car with her mother. 'It was fun, Mommy,' she chirped.

'I'll bet,' Sara agreed. 'I knew I should have sent your father to pick you up. He would really have enjoyed this. How much bail money shall I bring to the jail, Julie?'

Greg took one look at the fluorescent message on the sign he held, and laid it flat on the pavement, putting his foot into the middle of it and bending it double.

'That was a perfectly good sign till you ruined it,' Julie said. She pushed her wet hair back from her mud-streaked forehead. Leicester's leash slipped its knot and dropped from her wrist.

'Make yourself another one,' he suggested. 'It will give you something to do. Shall we go negotiate with the officer over what your car is worth?' He tugged her off towards the police car, then turned back to the foreman. 'Make yourself useful and call a wrecker to move that endloader,' he suggested.

'It would be easier just to—'

'Don't you dare start it up again,' Greg ordered. 'If it slid once, it can slide again. And stay here, guarding that car, until it's moved.'

'As long as no one has to put up bail,' Sara said

brightly, 'I think I'll take my offspring home and clean the mud off her. That, plus trying to figure out this scene, should keep me busy all weekend.' The little car signalled and started to pull out into traffic.

Kristen leaned out of the window and yelled, 'Bye, Leicester!'

The dog had been sniffing along the pavement, looking in vain for the playmate who had vanished so suddenly. At the shrill call, he raised his head, barked once, and started to lope after the car. He cut between Greg's feet, and the dangling leash caught on Greg's shoe, spinning him around and dumping him face-first on the concrete path. Julie grabbed for the leash and missed. She was already off balance because of Greg's tumble, and she landed on the cement atop him. He grunted as if the blow had knocked the breath from him.

The dump truck turning in off Grand Avenue didn't have a chance of missing Leicester. The truck swerved, and the brakes squealed, but Leicester didn't turn from his course. The right front wheel caught the dog a glancing blow and flung him across the concrete.

Julie sat up on the pavement and started to scream.

Leicester's brown eyes were cloudy, but he raised his head a bare half-inch as Julie approached.

'Don't touch him,' Greg warned.

Julie turned on him. 'Leicester would never bite me.'

'He's hurt, Julie. Right now he doesn't know—'

Leicester wagged his tail, weakly.

'Oh, he doesn't know me, does he?' Julie snapped.

'You poor baby,' she crooned to the dog. 'We have to get you to Dr Myers right away.'

Greg looked around. 'Hand me that sign,' he ordered the foreman, who was standing on the path, his hard hat in his hand and his mouth open. 'I think we can ease him on to it and carry him without hurting him worse. I'm afraid you'll have to hold him on your lap, Julie. My car isn't meant for cargo.'

The foreman scratched his head. 'You mean you're going to take the crazy dame and her dog to the vet? In that snappy car?'

Greg looked him over for a brief moment, and then said, 'If you don't learn to do as you're told without asking stupid questions, you're not only going to be looking for a new job, but for a dentist to put your teeth back in.'

The foreman considered that, and picked up the sign. Leicester yelped a little as they moved him. 'Sorry, old boy,' Greg muttered as he shifted Leicester's weight and slid him into the car. Julie soothed the animal, and he raised his head a little, and then closed his eyes and put his chin down on her hand. He was panting.

'Hurry!' she said.

'I'll do the best I can,' Greg said as he slid behind the wheel. 'It *is* rush-hour.'

Julie stroked Leicester's long ear. 'Did Kristen see it happen?'

'I don't think so. Sara didn't come back—I doubt she even realised what was going on.'

'Good,' Julie murmured. 'It wasn't Kristen's fault.

It was mine. I should have kept that leash in my hand, instead of tying it like that. But he just never strays—'

'Don't kick yourself. He could have gotten away from you anyway, Julie, or pulled you right along with him.'

'I should have left him at home.'

Greg didn't answer. He tapped his fingernails on the steering wheel at a red light, and took the first opportunity of turning off on to a side street where traffic was lighter.

'It's getting late,' she fretted. 'I hope Dr Myers is still there.'

'The cop knew which clinic you meant. He's going to call and have the vet wait for us. That man deserves a commendation.'

'The cop? For keeping his temper while dealing with me, I suppose you mean.' Julie's voice was sarcastic.

'No, that wasn't what I meant, as a matter of fact. But if being mad at me makes this easier for you, be my guest.'

'Why would I be mad at you? It wasn't your fault Leicester ran in front of a truck.'

'That's the first time you've absolved me of anything,' he murmured. 'Julie, this was no one's fault. Not yours, not Kristen's, not mine, not the truck driver's.'

The veterinary surgeon was a big man, with grey hair that looked as if it hadn't been combed in a decade. His enormous hands were gentle as he lifted Leicester to a stainless-steel table and began to examine him. He inspected Greg and Julie over the top of his half-rimmed glasses. 'You two look as though you've been through a war,' he said.

Greg fingered the triangular tear in the knee of his flannel trousers, and sighed. 'It sort of feels that way, too,' he said.

The dog yelped once, pitifully, and subsided.

'Can't you do something to stop his pain?' Julie whispered. She knew it wasn't fair, that it wasn't the vet's fault, and that he had to first find out what was wrong before he could do anything.

Dr Myers' blue eyes were compassionate. The man said nothing; his fingers never paused in their gentle exploration of Leicester's battered body.

Ashamed of herself, Julie looked down at her clenched hands. They were bloodstained, and her bruises were beginning to make themselves felt.

Finally, the vet straightened up with a sigh and shook his head. 'I can try,' he said. 'But he's badly hurt, and I wonder if I'd be doing him any favours. Julie, perhaps we should just let him go to sleep. It would be the compassionate thing to do.'

He looked at Greg with a world of meaning in his eyes. Greg nodded understanding and put his hands on Julie's shoulders, as if he was trying to send her his own strength.

She shook her head slowly, unbelieving, and sank into a chair in a corner of the treatment room.

'He's had a good long life, Julie,' the doctor said. 'He's been a faithful friend.'

Slow, hot tears brimmed in her eyes and then quietly overflowed, cutting scorching trails through the muddy streaks on her face. 'He's old,' she said, 'but he's strong. Surely—' She reached out to pet Leicester's head with a gentle finger, and he tried to lick her hand. It seemed to Julie to be a plea, his way of saying that he wasn't ready to die.

'You said you could try,' she said firmly. 'Please, Dr Myers, I want to give him every chance.'

The vet sighed. 'All right, Julie. He's your dog, and it's your decision. I'll give him the best I've got. But I can make no promises.'

'I know,' she said.

Greg bent over her and laid his face against her hair. She pulled his hand against her cheek.

It seemed hours later when they left the small clinic. But the surgery was over and, though Leicester had not yet awakened from the anaesthetic, he was alive, and that was more, Dr Myers admitted, than he had expected.

'I'm frankly amazed,' he said. 'But even if he comes through this all right—'

'He will,' Julie said stubbornly.

'He's very old, and he's not going to be around for ever. I think you should get another dog, Julie.'

She shook her head violently. 'No! I'll never have another dog. It's too hard on me when things like this happen.'

The doctor said gently, 'At least think it over, my dear.'

She turned at the door. 'Thank you, for staying late, and—everything.'

He nodded. 'Leicester's one of my favourite patients,' he said. 'We'll take care of him.'

In the car, she started to shiver violently. Greg

started the engine and leaned over to clasp both her clenched hands in his. She tried to pull herself together. 'I'm being silly,' she said. 'I've taken up a great deal too much of your time already.'

'It's not silly to fret when a good friend is in danger,' he said. The softness in his voice brought fresh tears, and great racking sobs seemed to tear her throat.

Greg smoothed her mud-stiffened hair back from her forehead and said something under his breath. He put the car into gear.

She didn't notice where they were going until he pulled into an echoing ramp and parked the car in a reserved slot. Then she looked around curiously. 'Where are we?'

'I thought you'd feel better if you could clean up and pull yourself together before you faced Randie,' he said.

Julie shook her head. 'She's spending the weekend at Sara's.' She wet her lips. He'd brought her to his apartment, of course. She should be upset about that, but she couldn't find it in her heart to care. She knew only that she could not face that silent, empty house tonight. 'I don't want to go home alone,' she said. Leicester's favourite rug in a heap in the pantry, his tennis ball lying in the garden, his leash hanging beside the back door... No, she remembered, his leash was on the floor of Greg's car, where she had dropped it on the way to the clinic. She kicked it aside, as if blaming it for the accident. Leicester might never need it again.

No, she told herself, you mustn't think that way. He'll be fine. He *has* to be.

'If I'd known that, I would never even have considered taking you home,' he said. 'You're right, you shouldn't be alone.' He came around the car to help her out.

Julie's stiff muscles protested.

'That was quite a fall you took,' he said.

'You had it worse. You hit the concrete, and then I smashed into you.'

'I must admit I'm feeling it,' he said. He held out a hand. Concrete dust was embedded in the scrapes that lacerated his palm. 'I'm not as young as I used to be. We must look like a pair of homeless waifs.' He talked gently all the way to his apartment.

She didn't even notice the colours, or the décor. The only thing she saw was that the room they entered was large and airy and full of light. The drapes were open to the western sky, and the rosy glow of a pink sunset poured across the carpet.

He led her across the room and down a short hall. 'Don't panic,' he said as he put a hand on the doorknob. 'But there's only one bath, and it's off my bedroom.'

She nodded. Who cared? she thought. If she could just get into a shower, and wash her hair… Anyone's bathroom would do, at a pinch.

'I'll go start the water,' he said. 'Here's a robe—not a good fit, I'm afraid, but the best I can do.'

She was obscurely pleased that he didn't have a wardrobe full of assorted women's clothes. Then she told herself not to be silly. All that meant was that his women friends brought their own things, and picked up after themselves. She carefully stripped off her filthy clothes, half-afraid that the hardened mud might cause them to break into pieces, and shrugged into the terry robe. It smelled a little like him, she thought.

The bathroom was already steamy. She thought at first her swollen eyes were playing tricks on her; she blinked and decided that it could not be her imagination. There really was a sunken, kidney-shaped tub in the middle of the bathroom floor, two steps down from the plush chocolate-brown carpet and surrounded by what looked like an acre of salmon-coloured ceramic tiles. Gold faucets at both ends gushed full streams of water, and mounds of bubbles rose above the edge of the tub.

'I was expecting a shower,' she said, and wondered whether he bought bubble bath by the gallon.

Greg shrugged. 'If you'd rather,' he said, 'there's one over there. But I thought a good soak would help your sore muscles.' He turned off the taps.

It looked good. 'Thanks,' she said. 'It was very thoughtful of you.' She felt a little shy, all of a sudden, standing there in his bathroom, wearing his bathrobe.

He said softly, 'Enjoy your bath.'

After he was gone, she stood there for a long minute, staring down at the bubbles. What about his sore muscles? she wondered, and then shrugged off the robe and climbed gingerly down into the water.

It was positively decadent. The water swirled around her, driven by tiny jets in the sides of the pool. She slid slowly under the surface of the water, letting the bubbles soak the muddy residue from her hair. When she could hold her breath no longer, she sighed and sat up, leaning back against the side of the tub to let the throbbing sensation of the water begin to drive the pain from her neck muscles. Her wet lashes fluttered, and then rested wearily on her cheeks.

The bathroom door opened. Julie's eyes snapped open and she slid down into the bubbles until her nose brushed the top of the foam.

'I brought you a glass of wine,' Greg said. 'I thought it would help you relax.'

'You brought two glasses of wine,' she corrected sternly.

'Well, yes.' He leaned over the edge of the tub and handed her one. 'I thought I'd wait in the bedroom, in case you went to sleep in here and tried to drown. It looks as though you've already made an attempt at it.' He retreated to the door. He was still wearing the trousers with the hole in the knee, she saw.

She felt faintly ridiculous. Here he was, trying to be helpful, and she was acting like an outraged virgin! He'd had a rough day, too, she reflected, and all because of her. And now, when he might very well want to be soaking away his own pain, guess who was occupying his bathtub and preventing him from using it?

I should hurry and get out, she thought. But the water was so comforting, the slick bubbles so soothing, that she wanted to stay there for ever.

'Greg,' she said. 'If you'd like to come in—' She started to blush, and hurried on. 'I mean, that knee has to be bothering you. And I'm not foolish enough to think that you might have any ideas—I mean, you couldn't possibly want to—I must look like sin,' she finished defiantly.

'If this is an invitation,' he said promptly, 'I accept.'

She primly averted her eyes, and it wasn't until he had leaned back in the tub opposite her with a satisfied sigh that she dared to look at him.

The bubbles should have made him look ridiculous, she thought. Men like Greg Roberts just didn't take bubble baths. But he had no trouble carrying it off. There would never be any doubt, she thought, about Greg's masculinity. He was simply so comfortable with himself that he didn't care what anyone else thought, and as a result, she concluded, men respected him, and women could swoon over him…

She was feeling a little light-headed herself.

'As for looking like sin,' he said, 'you do, as a matter of fact. You look very, very sinful. All you need is an apple, and you'd be the biggest temptation ever faced by man.'

'No hanky-panky in the tub,' she warned. 'You stay on your side, and I'll stay on my side.'

He grinned. 'I thought you just said I couldn't possibly want to do anything,' he teased.

'I haven't any idea what you want—'

'Don't you?'

It was a soft and sultry question, and Julie felt her insides start to squirm.

'You look very tired,' he said, quietly.

Relief, mixed with a curious twinge of disappointment, rippled through her. 'I didn't sleep last night,' she said. 'There was no breeze, and the house had gotten so hot—'

He frowned. 'I thought you had air-conditioning in that place.'

'It broke,' she said crisply.

'Why didn't you call me?'

'Why should I? So you could gloat about it?' She slid down in the water, luxuriating in the warm silkiness of the bubbles.

'No, so I could send a repairman over.'

'You keep one in your back pocket, perhaps?'

'No, dear. We've got so many buildings scattered around, and it's so hard to get good service, that I started my own division to take care of the heating and cooling plants. We've got people on call around the clock.'

Julie looked at him and considered dumping the rest of her glass of wine over his head, just for the sheer perverse pleasure of it.

'Why didn't you ever tell me that?'

'I had no idea you wanted to know. Shall I recite a list of everything that Roberts Development does?'

'Just send me a catalogue.'

'I'll get a repairman over there first thing tomorrow.'

'Not tonight?'

'Do you want to go let him in? I certainly don't.' He tipped his head to one side and regarded her thoughtfully. 'Feeling better?'

'My body, yes. The aches and pains are going away, and the scratches are all soaked clean. But the hole in my heart—' She shook her head. 'I don't think I'll ever forget that instant when I knew the truck couldn't miss him.'

'I think the doctor's right.'

'Another dog? Not you, too, Greg. It was my carelessness that nearly cost Leicester his life, and I don't want to be responsible again. Besides, no dog could take his place.'

'Nobody said he should. Another dog would find a new place in your heart.'

'There could never be another Leicester,' she said, and added, with more stubbornness than logic, 'Nothing is going to happen to him, anyway.'

He sipped his wine and set the glass aside. 'Dr Myers is the expert, and he's a whole lot less certain than you are. Do you know what this sounds like to me?' he asked pleasantly. 'Another case of Julie denying reality and hanging on to the past so hard that she's ignoring the beautiful things she could have in the present.'

'That's an unfair accusation!'

'Look, if you had told me you didn't want another dog because you were tired of coping with fleas, or because you were going to travel six months of the year and didn't want to board an animal, or because you just can't stand dogs any more, I could understand. But you're simply afraid to walk towards the future. You're so busy clinging to what was, that you're pushing aside everything that could be—'

She bent her head. Tears splashed into the bubbles.

'I'm sorry,' he said. 'I'm a heartless beast to talk to you this way.'

'That's right,' she sniffed. 'You're heartless, and a beast, and—'

'And correct,' he said. 'But we'll talk about that some other time. Why don't you tell me about Leicester?'

She didn't want to. But she found herself telling him

about the silly puppy that Leicester had been, and how she had found him under the Christmas tree the year she was twelve, and how he had got his name.

'I was in my Tudor period,' she said. 'I used to wander around pretending I was really a princess, and somehow I'd ended up here by mistake. It made me feel elegant, I suppose, to have a dog with an aristocratic name; there was nothing less graceful than me when I was twelve.'

'What were you like?' Greg asked lazily.

'I was about ten feet tall and six inches around, and my hair was always falling in my eyes, no matter what I did.'

'I don't believe a word of it.'

'It's all true. And,' she went on ruthlessly, 'my best friend had grown breasts that year, and I was jealous because I was still as flat as a plank.'

His eyes dropped a little, and he said unsteadily, 'I'll bet she's the one who's jealous now.'

Julie glanced down, and realised that the bubbles had been slowly dissipating. Her breasts gleamed just under the surface of the water, rising slickly with every breath, and then retreating coyly. As the bubbles vanished, the water became transparent. There was very little that Greg couldn't see.

'Oh, my God!' she whispered.

Greg gave her a crooked smile. 'I did agree to conditions when I got in here,' he said. 'Would you like to release me from my promise to stay on this side of the tub?'

She shook her head, uncertainly. 'I'm going to get out,' she announced.

'That's what I was afraid of,' he mourned. 'Foolish me, I could have kept right on enjoying the view.'

She scrambled out of the water and grabbed for his terry robe. Greg was right behind her. 'On the other hand,' he said, 'this could be fun, too.' He swooped up a big towel and enveloped her in it, rubbing her dry as if she had been a child.

Don't fight him, she thought. Don't make a fuss...

It felt good, and she stood still, her spine arched and her head tipped back, letting him rub her down with the fluffy towel. His hands slowed, and the movements of the towel became sensual caresses, patting her skin to a rosy glow that reflected the fire that had kindled deep inside her.

She had wanted him for days, but her doubts had nagged at her. He had seemed a selfish, self-centred man, determined on his course, no matter how many people he hurt. But he wasn't like that at all, she thought. The tender side of him, the part that had suffered with her, was a side he hid well. But she recognised it now, and her doubts were gone. They had vanished like the last puff of smoke from a bonfire, leaving only the embers, still scorchingly hot beneath the surface.

She stepped away from him deliberately. He let her go without protest, though the desires of his body were impossible to hide. She picked up a dry towel and turned to him. 'Turn about is fair,' she said softly.

She saw the startled pleasure in his eyes, and it urged her on. She used the lessons he had just taught her, and in mere minutes he said, hoarsely, 'You'd better stop, Julie.'

'What if I don't want to stop?'

'Then you're going to end up in my bed. I can't stand much more.'

She licked her lips, and knew that she was burning every bridge behind her. 'Good,' she whispered. She let the towel drop, and held out her hand to him.

CHAPTER EIGHT

IT WAS as though they had always been lovers. Julie seemed to know with some inborn sixth sense how to touch him, to caress him, in order to drive him past reason. But, if she was instinctively gifted at pleasing him, then Greg was expert at pleasing her, at inflicting upon her the exquisite torment that was making love: two bodies reaching together for promised perfection, two souls melding in a heart-stopping symphony that carried them beyond time, beyond place, to a world where only lovers dwelt.

And when the emotional upheaval was done, and they lay spent and breathless in each other's arms, she whispered, 'I'm sorry it wasn't emerald satin sheets.'

'It doesn't matter.' He kissed the hollow at the base of her throat, and traced the rise and fall of her breasts with a curious finger, and said huskily, 'There is an acre of emerald satin in your eyes.'

She rested her cheek against the curly hair on his chest, and listened to the steady thump of his heart as it slowed gradually towards normality. Her own heart, she thought, was about to burst from happiness. Never had everything been so perfect, each fragment of her life so completely in tune.

She tensed in his arms. Greg smoothed her tangled, still-damp hair, and whispered, 'What's wrong, my dear?'

'Leicester,' she said, on a sort of broken sigh. 'I forgot all about him. What if he dies, Greg? I caused it—'

And if he says, *Leicester is only a dog*, she thought, I am going to scream. I feel awful about Leicester's accident. How could I possibly have put him out of my mind, and abandoned myself to my own pleasure?

'He won't die. He wouldn't dare, with you depending on him.' Greg snuggled her closer in his arms, curving his body around hers, not in a sensual way, but as he would have cradled a hurt child. He held her close as she relived that aeons-long instant when she had seen the truck and the dog and had known what must happen. The strength of his arms soothed her, and she dozed, secure in the thought that Greg would watch over her.

It was grey dawn when the nightmare came, and she struggled to wake from it, knowing with the rational side of her mind that if she could only reach consciousness it would all come right again. Greg's strong fingers brushed the tears from her cheeks, and he said, with sleepy concern, 'Have you had a bad dream?'

She nodded strenuously. 'It was awful. I dreamed Leicester was hit by a truck.' Her eyes widened, as full wakefulness overtook her. 'But it wasn't a dream. It was true, wasn't it?'

'I'm afraid so.' He raised himself on one elbow and looked down at her. He stroked her hair, and traced the outline of her face with a gentle finger.

'I suppose you think it's silly to cry over a dog,' she said defiantly, sniffing.

'No,' he said. He kissed a tear away and settled back into the pillows, pulling her into the warm nest formed by his arms. 'Though I must admit I've never felt as you do. I never had a dog, you see.'

'Never?' She raised her head and peered at him in the dim light, and then settled back with a sigh. His shoulder was far from being a soft pillow, but his skin was smooth and warm, and she liked feeling the gentle play of his muscles against her cheek. 'Not even when you were little?'

He shook his head. His chin rubbed against her hair. 'My mother thought dogs were filthy nuisances. She absolutely refused to let me have one.'

So he hadn't always got everything he wanted. Julie smiled a little. 'You sound as if you're still angry about it.'

'Do I?' He looked at her curiously. 'I am, I suppose. I hadn't realised that. I thought I was long over it.'

'Didn't your father understand?' It was a soft question.

'My father,' Greg said deliberately, 'was too busy spending my mother's money on his girlfriends to have any interest at all in me.'

'Oh! That's rather awful.' Her voice was breathless; Greg's fingers had found her ribs and were innocently wandering over the satin skin.

'In a way, I can't blame him. There was a tremendous family resemblance between my mother and cousin Anita.' His hand slipped casually to her hip, and then rambled down the side of her thigh.

'But which problem came first?' Julie asked, willing herself to keep her wayward thoughts under control.

'I mean, was he unfaithful because she was—' She paused.

'A shrew,' Greg supplied.

His hand was sending mindless shivers of delight coursing through her veins. Julie drew an unsteady breath, and went on, a little hazily, 'Or did she get that way because he had other women?'

He removed his arm from under her head and laid her back against the pillows. 'I haven't the vaguest idea, Julie,' he said. 'And besides, who cares?' He bent his head to caress her breast, catching the tender tip playfully between his teeth.

'I only wondered,' she gasped. She tried to ignore the fire that was building in the pit of her stomach.

He raised his head and grinned at her. 'Then perhaps we should find something else for you to wonder about,' he whispered, and kissed the shadowy cleft between her breasts.

'I wonder how much of this I can stand before I fall apart into little pieces,' she confessed unsteadily.

'Is that a challenge?' His voice was muffled. He began drawing concentric rings around her nipple with the tip of his tongue.

Julie cried out and arched against him, trying to pull him down to her. He shook his head and smiled at her, his teeth gleaming white in the dimness. 'Oh, no,' he said. 'You can't seduce me that easily, Juliet. And I don't think you're going to disintegrate, either—not for a good long time.'

He taught her things about her body that she had never dreamed of. Time after time he took her to the brink of tantalising ecstasy, and then drew back, ignoring her breathless pleas for release, and paused a moment to let their heartbeats steady. Then he would begin again to find new sensitive locations and new ways to caress them, until Julie thought she would surely go mad with the pleasure of it all.

When finally the moment came when they did not pull back, it was as if the world dropped out from under them in a sudden, blinding flash, and left them to fall fearlessly through time and space while they celebrated the wonder of each other.

And when they rested again, still tangled together in the aftermath of passion, she looked at him with eyes that had suddenly cleared, and thought, of course, I've fallen in love with him. This is it; this is for ever. This is the man I want to spend my tomorrows with, until the end of time...

The aroma of coffee tantalised her nose, and she sighed and rolled over and buried her face in the pillow that still vaguely held his scent. The fragrance of bacon frying followed, and Julie pushed herself reluctantly out of bed. 'It may not be a romantic aftermath to a night of passion,' she mumbled to herself, 'but I'm starving.' And so, to judge by the smells, was Greg.

She hadn't paid much attention to the apartment the night before. Now she noted that the bedroom was large and airy and nearly empty, containing just the bed and a large, comfortable-looking chair. Not even a chest of drawers interrupted the expanse of chocolate-brown carpeting. Nothing was out of place, because there was nothing to be messed up.

She couldn't find her clothes. She checked the wardrobe without a great deal of hope. Not even Greg, she thought, was neat enough to have hung her yellow skirt up, in the condition it was in. The skirt, she seemed to remember, had been past salvation. Nevertheless, its absence left her with a problem—how was she to get back home, with nothing to wear?

She chewed on her bottom lip for a minute, and finally adopted his terry robe again, rolling the sleeves up to allow her hands free movement. It felt a little silly to be walking around swathed in the long robe on a hot, summer day. But she'd feel like a complete idiot if she dashed out to the kitchen in the altogether and found Greg there already wearing a business suit and a tie.

The rest of the apartment was nearly as bare as the bedroom was. It was all done in shades of brown and salmon, masculine colours and patterns, and big, comfortable pieces of furniture.

It's fortunate, she thought, that he doesn't have a lot of stuff. We won't have duplicates to argue about.

She caught her breath and scolded herself. It was foolish, she thought, to make any assumptions. Who ever said anything about moving in together? Greg certainly hadn't. There hadn't been time last night.

And there might not be any discussion of it this morning, either, she told herself sternly. Last night had been, in a sense, an accident. Greg had enjoyed himself, she had no doubt of that. But, this morning, he might well be anxious to get things back to normal. Even if he wasn't impatient to forget the passion of last night, that didn't mean he was eager to make this a permanent arrangement. Just because she had decided she wanted to spend her life with him didn't mean that *he* felt anything of the sort.

'Idiot,' she muttered under her breath. 'When you fall, you fall hard, and you don't even bother to find out if there's a safety net underneath.'

She swallowed hard. Well, she could play it as it came, she decided. She would enjoy the morning and, if that was all there was to be, then she would hold the memory of last night close in her heart and treasure it for ever. She could not insist on commitment, and she wouldn't even count on having a discussion of what the future was to be. She would savour the moment, and let tomorrow take care of itself.

'Because you're too chicken to ask him what his intentions are,' she accused herself. 'Because you've tumbled headlong in love with him, and you don't want to know if he's only playing games.' But she shook the concern off. There was nothing she could do about it, anyway.

The smell of bacon had masked some other delightful aromas, she decided as she trailed through the apartment. There was something that smelled like cinnamon, and there was a tangy citrus odour...

Play it cool, she ordered herself. 'Hi!' she called as she followed her nose into the kitchen. 'What do I have to do to get my clothes back?'

Greg was turning strips of bacon on a paper plate. He was wearing nothing but a pair of battered jeans, and her heart rocked as he said, 'Why? Are you in a hurry?'

'Not really,' she whispered. The sight of him, his

lean body tanned, the muscles flexing effortlessly in his arms, brought back all the longing and hunger of the night. The faint hope that perhaps she had imagined it all, that she had dreamed the idea of being in love with him, evaporated. He could still be the aggravating and arrogant man who had set her teeth on edge and made her swear to resist him. But he was also the gentle man who could share her pain. He was the passionate lover who could make her abandon inhibition, and he was the lonely little boy who had never had a dog, or even a father who cared about him…

And she loved every facet, every sliver of him. That, she thought humbly, was not going to go away.

'Well, Greg,' said a sneering male voice from the far corner of the kitchen, 'I never dreamed you would have to hide a—lady's clothes to keep her in your bed.'

Julie jumped a foot. She turned towards the sneer, unwilling to believe that she had heard it correctly. 'Keith!' she said incredulously.

He moved away from the door. 'Yes, it's me, Julie, dear. So you've found your way to Gregory's bed—I mean, heart.'

'That,' Greg said mildly, 'was uncalled for.'

Keith grinned. 'I wondered why you were so anxious for me to state my business and leave this morning, Greg,' he said. 'So anxious, in fact, that you haven't even asked me to sit down.'

'Keith, I never ask you to sit down,' Greg pointed out. 'I never encourage you to stay at all, or hadn't you noticed? I only let you in this morning because you'd put your foot in the door, and I didn't want to explain to Anita how I'd happened to cripple you.'

'Your generosity stuns me. I thought, of course, that there must be a lady in question,' Keith went on. 'But this *does* surprise me. You know, I didn't believe that scene you two played at Lynne's wedding. It was just a little too much to be real, don't you think?'

'Believe it, Keith,' Greg said cheerfully. 'Now, if you'd like to depart, Keith—'

'Oh, of course. I wouldn't want to interfere with your breakfast, or anything else you might be thinking about. You can let me know about that investment when you've had a chance to think it over, Greg.'

'I can let you know right now. The answer is no.' He ushered Keith out and closed the door with a determined bang.

Julie was standing by the refrigerator, her hands buried in the pockets of his robe. 'Keith's a real charmer, isn't he?' she said, bitterly.

He shot a look at her. 'Oh, quite.' He sounded preoccupied. 'Let's have breakfast in the living-room.' He reached for a tray and started piling things on it.

She bit her lip. What was worrying him? she wondered. Keith, and what tales he might spread throughout the family? If that was it, did it bother him for the sake of her reputation, or his own freedom?

'Where?' she asked as she led the way into the big living-room. There wasn't so much as a coffee table in sight.

'Over by the window. Or are your muscles too stiff to allow you to sit on the floor?'

'I am not a hundred and three years old,' she retorted, and dropped gracefully to a cross-legged pose on the carpet beside a pile of floor cushions. Let's keep it light, she told herself. Let's get through breakfast, and get the clothes back, and then…

'What did you do with my clothes?' she asked again.

He set the tray down between them and handed her a napkin. 'There's a dry-cleaning place downstairs. They'll be done in an hour or so.'

'You have a great deal of confidence in this establishment.' Suddenly, another possible explanation of his preoccupation occurred to her, and her heart seemed to jolt to a stop. Had Leicester made it through the night? Or had Dr Myers called, and Greg was even now trying to find a way to break the bad news to her gently?

'I should call the clinic,' she said, and started to get to her feet.

'I already did,' he said absently. 'Leicester is doing fine, and Dr Myers said he can come home in a few days. He sounded astounded, to be perfectly truthful. Would you like bacon? There's coffee cake, too, but it's only warmed up from frozen.'

Suddenly her appetite was gone. She sank back to the carpet, gratitude at Leicester's recovery mixing oddly with confusion. If it wasn't the dog, then what was causing this odd abruptness of Greg's? He had become a stranger, she thought, and she didn't know whether to be angry or sad. 'Just coffee, thanks,' she whispered.

His eyes had darkened. He looked at her once, quickly, and then away.

'You have a pretty view,' she said. She didn't know if it was pretty or not, only that she couldn't bear the silence.

He stared out of the window, and for a moment she thought he hadn't heard her. 'Most people like the east side of the building better,' he said. 'They can see the state capitol from there. But I've always liked this view in the mornings.'

'How long have you lived here?'

'A couple of years.' He saw her look around and added, 'I guess I never thought furniture was all that important.'

'I can see that.' She sipped her coffee. It hurt her throat to swallow.

'Look,' he said abruptly. 'I'm sorry, all right?'

She bit her tongue and stared down twenty storeys to the traffic crawling along the avenues. I don't want to hear this, she thought. To have what happened between them last night reduced to a casual fling would be more than she could bear.

He sounded angry. 'I should have kept Keith out this morning, even if I had to amputate his foot with a butcher knife. But I'd just been in to check on you, and you were sound asleep. I didn't dream you'd come in—'

'And give him a tremendous story to pass around at family cocktail parties,' she said bitterly.

'Hell, I don't care what he says. He can take it straight to my grandmother and it won't bother me. But I know it upset you that he saw you here.'

She looked at him, half stunned. 'You're sorry because of this morning?' she said. 'Not because you regret what happened last night?'

He looked as if she'd struck him. 'Regret last night?' he repeated in disbelief. 'You thought I was sorry about making love with you?'

It *did* sound ridiculous. She felt colour rise in her cheeks, and said defensively, 'Well, it's no dumber than you believing that I still care what Keith thinks of me!'

'You don't?'

'No.' Her cup tipped as he reached for her, and the hot liquid cascaded on to the floor.

'Never mind,' he said. 'The carpet's coffee-coloured.'

'Did you pick it with this in mind?'

'Not especially,' he murmured against her throat. 'But I think it was an inspired choice.'

The empty cup slipped from her fingers and rolled gently across the floor. He kissed her thoroughly, sending violent shudders of pleasure surging through her body. 'Shall we make love now, or wait till after breakfast?' he asked finally, with a breathless unsteadiness in his voice.

Her eyes fell before the unabashed desire in his. 'Breakfast first,' she said. 'I'm starving.'

'You said you only wanted coffee.' He popped a bite of coffee cake into her mouth.

'My image,' she said, through the crumbs. 'I didn't want you to think I was a pig.'

'I think you've got a lot of self-control,' he mused. 'Of course, you're not sitting here looking at the same view I am.'

The wrapped robe had come loose, she saw, and the neckline now extended nearly to her navel. She smiled sweetly at him and rearranged it, making it more modest by about a half-inch. Then she leaned back against a cushion and picked up a crisp piece of bacon.

'Enjoy the scenery,' she suggested. He groaned, and she added, 'Self-discipline is good for your immortal soul, Greg.'

'It had better be,' he said. 'It's certainly hell on the rest of me.'

The cleaners had got the stains out of her skirt, but nothing could ever restore the colour to its original brilliance. However, she decided, it would get her by. 'Have you made any plans for today?' she asked as she smoothed the collar of her blouse.

'Does that mean you have?' Greg countered. 'Because I warn you, I don't dress up on weekends.'

'I only thought that since you were responsible for putting my car out of commission—'

'Why do I think I'm not going to like this?'

'I was supposed to go out to a flea market today.'

'Do you sell a lot of fleas at that shop of yours?' he asked, with apparent interest. 'I don't think I've ever been to a flea market.'

Julie tried to ignore the shivers that raged through her at the merest brush of his hand. 'Then you should start right away,' she said. 'You have no idea of what you're missing.'

The flea market was being held in a huge, old, barn-like structure in a small town a few miles outside of Des Moines. Greg stopped in the doorway and looked across the rows of tables, each piled high. 'All this stuff is valuable?' he asked, incredulously.

'It's valuable to someone.' She paid their admission fee.

'Sorry,' he said. 'I got so carried away I forgot to be a gentleman.'

'You're my guest.'

'Do you buy a lot of things here?'

Julie shook her head. 'Hardly ever.'

'So you just wander around and look?'

She smiled up at him. 'That's about it. It's my hobby, you see, as well as my job. In fact, I've had to make a private rule that I don't buy anything for myself at shows like this. Otherwise, I'd have bankrupted myself long ago.'

He didn't seem to be listening. He was standing beside a table of antique construction tools, seemingly lost in contemplation of what his trade had been like a hundred years ago. Julie smiled inwardly; perhaps Greg was more interested in the pioneering days than he would admit. She moved on slowly down the long aisles, making a note here and there, stopping to chat with a dealer.

He caught up with her at a velvet-covered table on which gemstones sparkled. She was admiring a jet bracelet which lay on a white velvet display board, and as he came up the aisle she stroked the silky black beads and regretfully shook her head. 'I can't go that high, I'm afraid,' she said. 'But if you'd like to think about it, and call me—' She handed her card across the table and linked her arm into Greg's. 'A passion for jewellery is one of the vices I inherited from Aunt

Rosa,' she said with a smile. 'Fortunately, I don't have the money to indulge myself, or I'd really be in trouble. I'm afraid I wouldn't know where to stop.'

'That was only a trinket,' he said.

'It's a fair price, but I couldn't get any more than that from it. If I can't add a mark-up, it doesn't make any sense to buy it.'

'Not even if you want to wear it?'

'It violates my rule,' she reminded.

'Well, it doesn't violate mine,' he said, and dragged her back to the table.

'Greg, I didn't mean—I wasn't trying to manipulate you into buying it for me. Gregory, stop it!'

He ignored her. When he turned away from the table a moment later with the bracelet in his hand, he looked down at her with a half-smile. 'Are you going to wear it, or shall I?' he asked. 'I think I'd look a bit silly, but if you really don't want it—'

'Of course I want it, you idiot.' She put her hand out, and he fastened the clasp and then pressed his lips to the pulse point inside her wrist. 'Thank you, Greg.'

'Keep looking at me like that,' he warned, 'and we'll have to find a more private place to discuss it. It's getting a little warm for comfort in here.'

'Warm,' she said, and snapped her fingers. 'That reminds me. We were going to call your air-conditioning people this morning.'

'I did,' he said with a grin. 'While you were getting dressed.'

'But they can't get in.'

'No, but Sara and Randie can. I called them this

morning, too. By the time you get home, the pesky thing will be fixed.'

He was obviously proud of himself. I wonder, Julie thought, if he realises that leaving the air-conditioning broken would have made me more likely to give in and sell the place?

Or did he mean, she wondered with a fluttering hope in the pit of her stomach, that he had changed his mind about wanting it, after all? Had he come to understand her determination, and was this his way of telling her he was sorry?

It was late afternoon by the time they reached the house again. Only then did Julie remember that she'd left some of the windows open when she and Kristen had walked up the street with their picket signs. She gave a thankful little shudder that it hadn't poured with rain overnight, and hoped that no opportunistic house-breaker had happened along before Randie got home.

Randie was in the kitchen, putting together an elaborate salad. A cool night at the lake seemed to have restored her, Julie thought. She looked better than she had in ages—younger, more interested in life.

'It's fixed, Juliet,' she sang out as they came in. 'Greg's nice men came this morning, and in just a little while—' Her pale blue eyes focused on their clasped hands; Julie tried to slip her fingers unobtrusively out of Greg's, but he refused to let her go.

Randie made no comment about it, however. 'It's still a little stuffy in here, though,' she said. 'I'm sure it will take all day to really get back to normal.'

'It feels wonderful to me—the flea market was hot. I want a shower before we go out,' she told Greg.

'Oh, is Greg taking you out to dinner? That's nice, dear. I even feel like cleaning a bit today,' Randie went on. 'It will be sort of fun, since it will probably be the last time.'

The cheerful words hung in the sunny kitchen like an ominous pall of smoke. 'Would you like to explain that, Randie?' Julie asked.

Greg shifted uneasily from one foot to the other. 'Perhaps I could—'

'Randie said it,' Julie pointed out. 'She can explain it.'

Randie looked from one of them to the other. 'Oh, dear,' she said unhappily. 'Perhaps I shouldn't have said anything. I thought surely by now you'd have told her—'

'Told me what?' Julie's voice cracked.

Greg shook his head. 'I haven't had a chance.'

'You've only had all day,' Julie said sarcastically. 'Whatever it is that you didn't want to tell me—is it something about the house?'

'Yes,' Randie said, delighted that her niece was so quick to comprehend. 'Gregory came up with a compromise, you see, so I can have my little apartment, after all.'

Julie couldn't swallow.

Randie said cheerfully, 'Isn't he wonderful to do that? He's bought my half of the house!'

CHAPTER NINE

THE air in the kitchen, it seemed to Julie, was suddenly heavy and threatening. Her heart pounded so hard that with every beat it jolted painfully against her breastbone. Every muscle in her body was so taut that it seemed that she would shatter into a million fragments.

'I suppose you're going to explain that you forgot to tell me?' she said to Greg. Her voice was amazingly calm.

'Not exactly. I thought you might take it like this, and I didn't want to ruin the fun we were having.'

'No, I don't imagine you did!'

'Julie, please, let me explain.'

'What is there to explain? You've been after my house in any way you could manage. Last night was—' Her voice broke. She swallowed hard and went on, 'It was just another route to get what you wanted!'

'Julie!' He reached out to her. 'I can't believe you're being so inflexible!'

She sidestepped his hand. 'No, Greg. No more fancy tricks. So you think you've gained an advantage by buying Randie's half. What are we going to do next? Shall we build a wall down the middle so you can bulldoze your half without interfering with my side? Or would you rather have title to the top floor, so you can bring a crane in and take it off?'

'I don't intend to—'

'Because I warn you, Greg Roberts, if you set foot in my half of this house, you're going to be arrested for trespassing!' She was almost sobbing. Randie hovered beside her, stunned by the havoc she had unwittingly caused.

'Julie.' His voice was low, steady. 'Listen to me. Last night was not a trick, nor was it a scheme.'

'Do you expect me to believe that you bought Randie's half out of the goodness of your heart?' The sarcasm in her voice was shrill. 'Perhaps you're going to give me the deed, in some grand gesture of chivalry!'

He sighed. 'Don't be ridiculous! I'm a businessman, Juliet, not a romantic. I need this bit of land—'

'If you think that owning half of this house on paper makes it any more likely that you will ever own the rest of it, you are dead wrong.'

'Julie, if you'd only listen—I didn't plan for it to happen this way.' He looked confused, as if she had suddenly turned into a spitting cobra.

'I have no sympathy for your mistakes. Get out of my kitchen.'

Silence reigned for a long instant. A muscle jerked in his cheek, but his voice was calm as he said, 'Don't you mean *our* kitchen, Juliet?'

'When you've got the paperwork to prove it, send your attorney over with it. In the meantime, I'd advise you to stay away from here, Greg.' She turned away from him and paused at the door. 'By the way,' she said, 'I won't need this to remind me of our beautiful time together.' She unclasped the jet bracelet from her wrist and threw it at him.

The old thread holding the bracelet together broke, and black beads showered Greg. Julie knew that later she would cry over the destruction of the collector's item, but she was too angry at the moment to care. She ran up the back stairs and slammed her bedroom door.

How could he? she was sobbing inside. All of his tender care last night, all of the friendly companionship today, all of the passion that lurked just under the surface when they touched each other—it was all false, all planned, all organised to push her off her guard. And all the time he had been scheming behind her back.

She flung herself across her four-poster bed and buried her face in the ruffled pillow-case.

All men are alike, she screamed inside. And you're lucky, Julie Gordon, to have found out about this one when you did, while you can still escape from his attraction...

It was a nice sentiment, but in the next few days she was compelled to admit that it did not have the force of truth behind it. For she could not escape from Greg. He seemed to have taken her warning to heart, for he did not appear at the house, or even next door, where the demolition of the concrete car park went on at an agonisingly slow pace. But, despite his physical absence, there was no getting away from him. He haunted her dreams, making her shiver with the sensation of those knowing hands upon her. When she walked through the old house, he seemed to be standing just around every corner, barely out of her sight. And sometimes it seemed she could actually hear his voice, the tone of it so clear that she was certain he was there.

She woke up sometimes in tears, and it was during one of those long nights that she admitted to herself that she would never get over Greg. There was no forgetting a man who had touched her heart so deeply.

But that didn't mean that she had to continue to be a fool, she told herself fiercely. It was time to pick up the pieces, to assess what she had learned, and to go on.

Perhaps that was why she listened to Dr Myers' request the day he told her Leicester could come home. 'I've got a puppy,' he said. 'The owners dumped him off here, and—'

'I told you I don't want another dog.'

'I know that.' He sounded exasperated. 'But I need a favour. I can't just keep him here in the clinic, and my boarding facilities are full. It's vacation season, you know.'

'What do you expect me to do about it?'

'I've got a new home lined up for him, but the people are going away for a while and don't want to cope with a pup until they get back. I wondered if you'd take him for a few days, just till they get back from their vacation.'

'How long is a few days?' Julie asked warily.

'Two weeks at the outside. I'd take him home myself, Julie, but my German Shepherds would eat this morsel alive. He's only eight weeks old.'

Julie sighed. She *did* owe the man a favour, after all, for the way he had taken care of Leicester. 'All right, I'll look at him. But I don't do nursing, you know.'

'He's a perfectly healthy pup. He's just too little—'

'I know. I heard you.'

The dog turned out to be a tiny, lop-eared basset puppy whose skin looked nine sizes too large for him. Like all of his breed, his ears dragged when he walked, his head drooped wearily, and he looked as mournful as though he had lost his only friend.

'What's his name?' she asked the vet.

'He doesn't have one yet. They're thinking about it while they're on vacation.'

'Some dog owners these people are going to be,' Julie grumbled, 'if they don't even have a name for him.'

The vet shrugged. 'So give him one,' he said. 'They can change it when they get home, if they want.'

She looked down at the sad-eyed dog. 'The doctor's right, you know,' she announced. 'I'm going to have to call you something. I can't go around for a week saying, "Here, you." So what's it going to be?'

The puppy tripped over thin air, as far as Julie could see, and rolled head over heels. He got up and shook his head and started off again. Julie laughed at him and said, 'I've never seen such an ungraceful animal! Maybe I should call you Dudley.'

She tried it out; the name had a comfortable feel, and the puppy seemed to think it was all right.

'Dudley?' the vet asked doubtfully. 'It does seem to fit him, I guess, but I can't think where you got it.'

Julie didn't explain. She scooped the puppy up and took him home. He lolled in her arms as she carried him into the house, his tongue making random swipes across her arms and her face until she got him settled in a makeshift pen in the corner of the kitchen. 'Don't get any ideas,' she warned him. 'This is not your permanent barracks.'

But it was fun to have a puppy around again. Kristen adored him, and soon taught him to respond when she called. Julie tried to explain the details of her arrangement with Dr Myers, but Kristen refused to believe that the puppy was only a house guest. She would run through the garden with Dudley at her heels, and dissolve in giggles when he took a spill and rolled over and over in the dust.

Leicester accepted the young intruder with good grace, though it seemed to Julie as if his long basset face looked more confused than usual, as if he didn't quite understand why Dudley should have been inflicted on him. But after the first few days, as Leicester continued to get well, Julie often found them curled up together, the old dog and the puppy, napping the long afternoons away as they waited for her to take them for a walk.

So the days went by, and soon it was a week since she had seen Greg. His absence had not lessened the pain. Randie had said nothing more about the sale of her half of the house, and Julie was afraid to approach the topic, for fear of the questions Randie might ask. The woman wasn't a dunce, after all, and Julie would just as soon not deal with her aunt's well-meant sympathy over the break-up of her romance.

Romance, she told herself. Twice she had been burned at the game of love. She would know better than to ever risk it again.

But she couldn't help noticing that Randie didn't laugh as much these days, and that her face was shadowed, and that she looked at Julie with ill-concealed concern in her eyes.

Annabel Hastings called one afternoon and invited her to tea. Julie refused as politely as she could, saying that the press of business would keep her in the shop.

'Gregory's out of town, if that makes a difference,' the old woman said bluntly.

'It doesn't,' Julie said crisply. Obviously, she thought, I didn't do too good a job of hiding my feelings last time I went to tea.

It didn't seem to bother Annabel Hastings. 'In that case,' she said, 'I'd like to have you come to my birthday celebration next Saturday. My family and friends will be coming in the evening for champagne and cake. It's nothing elaborate, just an old lady's party, but I'd like to have you there.'

'I'm sorry,' Julie said, stiffly polite. 'Thank you for the invitation, but I won't be able to attend.'

'Lynne will be back from her honeymoon by then. I'm sure she'd like to see you.'

Then she can come and see me at the shop, Julie wanted to say. 'If you'll excuse me, Mrs Hastings, I have a customer, and I need to get back to her.' She put the phone down with relief.

Had she already been in love with Greg, she wondered, on that afternoon in Annabel's lavender drawing-room? Had she already known then, deep inside, that this was the man she wanted, the man she could love for ever?

But that afternoon, she reminded herself, Annabel had not wanted Greg to leave with Julie. She had kept him by her side that day, and Julie had never expected to hear from the woman again.

So why had Annabel Hastings issued this new invitation? So that she could warn her off? To show her that Julie could never fit into the Hastings family? To tell her that Greg might be interested in an affair, but he could never be serious about a woman like Julie Gordon?

As if I needed to have that spelled out for me! Julie told herself drily. I'm not a fool.

Sara looked concerned. 'There's no customer waiting for you, Julie,' she pointed out.

Julie shrugged. In fact, she thought, business had never been worse. She didn't know whether to blame the dust and destruction next door, or the normal business cycle, or her own lack of enthusiasm. Somehow, it just wasn't as much fun any more.

'Are you going to the flea market this weekend?'

Julie shrugged. 'I don't think so.'

'Why not?'

'I've been to a lot lately. They've all got the same things.'

Sara looked disgruntled. 'You've missed two in the last week.'

Julie didn't argue. It was true, but she didn't realise that Sara had been counting. She wondered what the woman would say if she told the truth, if she said that, without Greg, nothing seemed to be any fun.

'You're just sitting there staring into space,' Sara said. 'What's wrong, Julie?'

'Nothing. Why don't you bring Kristen over to stay with me this weekend?' she said.

'Are you trying to change the subject?'

'No. I'll go back to the markets when the weather cools off.'

Sara looked unconvinced. 'We were talking about whatever is bothering you, not just the flea markets,' she pointed out, and sighed. 'But if you don't want to discuss it, I guess no one can force you. Kristen can't come, I'm afraid. She's going camping with my parents this weekend.'

Julie was genuinely sorry. At least with Kristen she could relax and be herself, she thought. The child took Julie's mind off her own troubles, and it was a relief not to have to watch out for prying eyes all the time.

Sara went into the drawing-room to unpack a new assortment of fancy quilted cushions. Julie began to rearrange a display of new monogrammed stationery in the small sitting-room. Through the heavy double doors, she could see Sara as she placed the cushions on the antique love-seat and arranged them just so. Then she looked up with a smile at a customer who had apparently just come in the front door. 'May I help you?' she said.

'Is Julie in?'

At the sound of the man's voice, every muscle in Julie's body tensed. I don't need this kind of trouble today, she thought. What on earth does Keith Evans want here?

She met Sara in the doorway. 'I'll take care of this,' she murmured.

Sara raised an eyebrow, obviously curious about Julie's tone of voice. 'I'll stay within earshot in case you scream,' she said softly.

'Hello, Keith. Are you looking for an anniversary gift for Anita?' Julie asked.

He laughed. 'I hadn't thought of that, actually. What would you recommend?'

'We have some pretty music boxes, just in from Italy.' She moved across to the display.

Keith lagged behind, watching the elegant swing of her slim hips. 'You know, I'm not surprised at Greg,' he mused. 'You always were a sexy little dish.'

She looked through him as if he hadn't spoken, and lifted the lid of a carved wooden box to let the tune ripple through the room.

'Of course, he may have pushed his luck this time,' Keith went on. 'There are a few people who don't think you'd be an appropriate choice for him.'

'I'm sure you're one of them, Keith. Do you think Anita would prefer a porcelain box? I've always liked this one best.'

'I think you're playing out of your league, Julie. Greg can be a dangerous proposition.'

Greg, dangerous? She wanted to laugh at how right Keith was, and how wrong his reasoning had been. Greg didn't set out to hurt people; the danger with him lay instead in his charm, in the fact that she wanted so badly to make him happy that she hadn't stopped to think about the consequences to herself until it was almost too late.

'You should drop him before he hurts you,' Keith went on, in that low, insinuating tone.

'And do what? Take up with you again?'

He seemed puzzled by the cynicism in her tone. 'You know where you stand with me,' he pointed out.

'That's right, nowhere at all. Goodbye, Keith. Don't come back.'

He flushed with anger. 'Perhaps you should consider this, Julie. Have you thought about your aunt? I'm sure you wouldn't want her to hear about what I saw that morning in Greg's apartment. She'd probably fall over on the spot and have a heart attack.'

'Blackmail, Keith?' she said gently. 'I never dreamed you'd resort to that. Isn't your love-life going well?'

He sputtered a little. 'You'll be sorry you turned me down.'

'I might,' she said thoughtfully. 'And then again, I might not. On the whole, I'm willing to take my chances.' She pointed to the front door, and as he reached it she added, 'I would advise that you not tell Randie anything unless you want Anita to have the details of this conversation, Keith. That's the bad part of blackmail, you see; you can't be successful at it unless your own past is free of shadows.'

When he had disappeared, she sank into a rocking-chair and put her head back against the needlepoint cushion. She felt suddenly exhausted, as if she'd been battered. My God, she thought, how did I ever convince myself that I loved that man? How did I get through two years in his company without ever seeing how cheap and shallow he is, how crude? How dare he come in here and say those things about Greg? He will never be worth a quarter as much as Greg.

My Greg, she thought, and clenched her hands against the pain. The man who held me while I cried out my pain. The man who taught me that I'm only half alive if I'm not beside him…

She opened her eyes slowly, warned by a subtle sixth sense that she was not alone. For a moment, she thought it was her imagination that had put him there, standing in the doorway between hall and drawing-room.

'Greg,' she said, in a husky whisper. Her heart was singing at the sight of him, drinking in every line of his face, every stitch of his well-tailored, coffee-coloured suit. She wanted to run across the room and throw herself against him. 'Your grandmother said you were out of town.'

'I got back early.' It was casual enough, but she saw the flicker in his eyes at the mention of his grandmother, and it brought pain to her heart.

He's afraid, she thought, that I might have called Annabel, and he's afraid of what I might have said. 'She invited me to her birthday party,' she said, and then could have kicked herself for explaining it to him. She didn't owe him any explanations, that was sure. With an effort, she tugged herself back to reality. Nothing had changed, she reminded herself. 'I asked you not to come back here,' she said.

He reached for the first thing he saw, one of the quilted cushions Sara had just arranged. 'You can't throw out a paying customer,' he said. 'I want to buy this.'

'For your living-room, I suppose?' There was an ironic twist to her words.

'Why not?'

'Because the cushion is green and mauve. Your living-room is brown and gold.'

'So I'll give it to someone.'

'Fine. It's twenty dollars. Do you want it gift-wrapped?'

'Don't be in such a hurry. I'm still looking.'

There was a tiny tinge of humour in this, she decided. This is an unusual kind of business you're running these days, Julie, she chided herself. You threw your last customer out, and you're doing your best to get rid of this one, too!

'Did the body shop get the dent in your car fixed properly?'

She nodded. 'They brought it back last night. I can't even see where the damage was.'

He picked up a wreath of dried flowers. 'I'll take this, too.'

'There's a smaller one over there.'

'I want the big one.'

Julie shrugged. 'It's all right with me. I just thought that you should know that you can kill as much time by buying a small item as an expensive one.'

'Do you think I'm cheap?'

'No, I think you're crazy. What do you want to talk about, anyway? Obviously you're here for a reason, and to gaze at my pretty face isn't it.'

His eyes focused suddenly on her face, and Julie's stomach felt as if the floor had dropped out from under her. It had been a careless comment, but there was nothing careless about the scrutiny he was giving her, or the longing in her heart. How badly she wanted to turn into his arms, to take that silly wreath out of his hand and throw it away so that he could devote all his attention to her.

She licked her lips nervously, and said, 'Well?'

'You've lost weight.'

'Have you started a new career as a carnival barker?' It was tart, mainly because he was right—in the last week, she had unintentionally pared an extra five pounds off an already slender frame.

'Have you been having second thoughts?' Greg's tone was soft, gentle, and deadly. 'We had something special, Juliet.'

Funny, she thought, that when he called her that, with the sensual twist that only he could give it, she didn't mind at all...

'I don't understand,' he whispered. 'How can you even think of turning your back on what we've shared?'

I could ask the same thing of you, she thought painfully. She swallowed hard to keep herself from answering, then said, trying to get back on to safe ground, 'I haven't had a bill for the repair of the air-conditioner yet.'

He sighed, and made a sort of helpless gesture. His eyes had not left her face, and the scrutiny was making her nervous.

'When it comes, I'll make sure you get your half,' she said.

'I may not own half the house by then. Randie

wants to back out of the deal. It was only a verbal agreement—'

'I can't think why you would have made that mistake.'

'I didn't have time to pin her down before she told you.' He sounded a little disgusted with himself.

'At least now I know why you came today.'

'Julie, don't be so damned stubborn. You don't need the house, anyway.' He came towards her. She backed slowly away, afraid that if he touched her she would lose all sense of reason.

'I don't?' It was only a whisper.

He brushed a loose strand of black hair behind her ear. His touch seemed to make her skin sizzle, and she shied away from him. Suddenly, he seemed to regain all of his arrogant confidence. 'Of course not,' he said. 'I'm not going to give up on us, Julie. What happens to us when we're together doesn't come to everyone, and you can't ignore that fact for ever. We're going to be spending all our time together, anyway. It will only complicate things if we have two places.'

'I wasn't aware we'd made any such arrangements.' She couldn't go any further; she was flat against the wall as it was.

He dropped a gentle kiss on her right eyebrow. 'We didn't exactly talk about it,' he admitted. 'There were other—more effective—ways of communicating what we wanted.'

She closed her eyes. 'So you're asking me to move in with you.'

He nodded. 'Isn't that what you want, darling?' His voice was soft, husky.

Under any other circumstances, she thought, I would love it. I would move in with you so fast that your head would be spinning. But not this way. What happens in a month or two, once the house is gone? Is it me you want, Greg, or only these four walls?

'I'll have to talk to Randie,' she murmured.

His hand brushed her cheek.

She felt her resolution slipping, and knew that she had to test him. She said, deliberately, 'She's being rather silly. She might as well sell you her half and have the money. It won't make any difference to me.'

He seemed to freeze. 'What do you mean?'

She opened her eyes and looked straight into his. 'I mean that you can't tear down half a house, and I have no intention of signing over my half, no matter what inducements you offer. You'll eventually learn that I can't be bought.'

For a long instant, there was a silence between them that seemed to chill the room. It gave her the answer she had needed. It was over. Her heart felt cold.

She said, almost gently, 'Did you really think that sexual attraction would be enough, Greg?'

'It was enough last weekend,' he said. His voice was heavy, lifeless.

She shook her head.

'I'm not trying to cheat you, Julie,' he said. 'I've offered you a price that is more than fair.'

'It's not a matter of price. I just want you to leave me alone.'

'Has it occurred to you,' he said, 'that you may never be free of me?'

Of course it has, she thought. I'll always love you.

But that doesn't change the fact that you've tried to manoeuvre me into doing what I don't want to do, that you've seduced me in an effort to get what you want.

'Is that a threat?' she asked calmly.

'I'm afraid not.' He paced the room and turned back to her. 'I must have been out of my head that night. It's quite possible—or haven't you even thought of it?—that you're carrying my child.'

If he had struck her, he couldn't have shocked her more. Her hand clenched convulsively on the dried-flower wreath, crumbling some of the blossoms into dust. Then she gathered her wits and said, 'Don't worry, Greg. There are ways of preventing that complication, and I would have no hesita—'

He grabbed her arm and swung her around. 'Don't fool yourself into thinking it would be easy. I would have a few things to say about that.'

Her breath was coming quickly and shallowly. She forced herself to laugh. 'Oh, for heaven's sake, Greg. Let's not get into a quarrel about a hypothetical child. It's a remote chance, at worst.'

She had caught herself in time; she had almost said, *at best.* My God, she thought painfully, I would give my life to have his child, and to have him love me as I love him…

'Please,' she whispered. 'Please just go away.' She turned blindly away from him and found her way down the hall.

Randie was in the kitchen, putting Dudley's dinner dish on the floor. The puppy yelped hysterically at the sight of Julie, and wagged his stubby tail. When he was ignored, however, he quickly settled down to the serious business of eating.

'You shouldn't have backed out of the sale,' Julie said.

Randie looked her over and sighed. 'He's been here, then?'

'Yes.'

'And you didn't reach an agreement?'

'No.' It was a bare whisper. Julie reached into the refrigerator, more to hide her face than because she wanted anything. She had thought she could keep her head, but now she felt as if she was going to dissolve into tears at any moment.

'I so hoped that you would find a way to compromise,' Randie said. She sat down in her favourite rocker in the corner of the kitchen. 'When you came in last Saturday, it was obvious how both of you felt.'

'Oh?' Julie said drily.

'Yes, dear. It was the way you looked at each other, and the way you couldn't keep your hands off each other.' She rocked gently, the chair creaking rhythmically. 'Don't look shocked at me, my dear. Of course I knew you'd spent the night with him.' It was calm. Then she added primly, 'The fact that I have never been married does not make me wholly ignorant of human emotions, Juliet.'

'It didn't bother you?' Julie asked curiously.

'You're an adult. And it was painfully evident that you didn't consider it to be a casual affair. No, it didn't bother me.' But she frowned. 'I must admit, though, when two people are so evidently attracted to each other, it's a sin when something as unimportant as a house keeps them apart.'

The words seemed to echo through Julie's head. *Something as unimportant as a house...*

Had she done the right thing? If it came to a choice between having Greg and keeping the house, had she been absolutely idiotic to give up the man she loved?

That's not the right question, she told herself breathlessly. The question really is, could I still be happy a year from now, or ten years, with a man who didn't respect my wishes, who didn't even try to understand something that was so dreadfully important to me?

'There are other houses, Juliet,' Randie said.

Something deep inside Julie seemed to blow into fragments with the force of a stick of dynamite. 'It's not the house,' she said, her voice rising on each word. 'It is not the damned house! It's the fact that he doesn't *care* that the house is important to me. Even if I gave up the house, it wouldn't work. Randie, he just doesn't give a damn, as long as he gets what he wants.'

Randie rose, with the dignity of age. 'And what about what *you* want, Juliet?' she said quietly, and left the room.

Julie sank down on the floor beside the puppy's bed. Dudley climbed awkwardly out of his blanket and into her lap. His warm body snuggled against her and his wet tongue lapped at her face.

'It would never work,' she said. 'It would be like a poison between us, always there, always building up, until eventually my love for him died of it. How long could I be happy with a man who doesn't respect what

I stand for? How can I love a man who doesn't care about the things that are important to me?'

But she did. That, she decided bleakly, was the worst part of it—that she loved him anyway.

CHAPTER TEN

THE heat-wave had finally broken and, though it was warm in the garden in the late afternoon, it wasn't the breathless, blistering heat of the holiday weekend just two weeks before.

How very much has changed since then, Julie thought as she sat on the back steps and watched while Dudley rambled through the dusty flowerbeds in search of entertainment.

The puppy bumped against a rosebush, and the dust that cascaded off the leaves made him sneeze. She laughed at him, and he bounded off to chase a house-fly.

But even the dust, she thought, was reaching the end. The jackhammers had fallen silent a couple of days ago, and the last of the rubble of the concrete car park had been hauled away. Now it was only bare, powder-dry dirt, with no activity and no sign as to what would happen next.

Nothing's going to happen, Julie told herself. Nothing can happen as long as I'm here.

She wondered what Greg would do with the property. He couldn't build on it—at least, nothing that was near his original plans—and he was unlikely to find a buyer for it. Would the land just be left to grow up in weeds, or to lie there barren, to be a reminder of him each time she looked out her bedroom window?

It seemed sometimes that the empty lot might be the only reminder she had of him. She hadn't even seen his little red sports car at the site of the new office building, though she couldn't help but look for it each time she and Dudley walked past.

She hated herself for even looking. She knew that she had made the only choice she could, the only one that made sense. But sometimes she still wished that it was possible to go back to that first night, to their first kiss in the courtyard at the Botanical Centre, before the house had come into it at all.

If, that night, she had known what was to come from that chance meeting, would she have turned and run? Probably not, she thought. Even then, he had held a magical attraction for her, something that could not have been ignored.

She looked down at the lavender notepaper dangling from her fingers. It had come in yesterday's mail, and she had been reading it over and over since. 'My dear Juliet,' Annabel Hastings had written, 'I don't want to pester you with the invitation, but I would like you to know that I really want you to come to my birthday party on Saturday.'

A straightforward note, with no explanation. And today was Saturday. Julie looked at her watch. In another few hours, the party would begin.

'And I,' she said, 'would love to be there, Annabel. But I'm not crazy enough to go.'

She wondered, with a tiny pain in her heart, if there would be a girl there—a pretty girl, of course, it would always be a pretty girl—who would catch Greg's eye, as Julie herself had at the Botanical Centre on the night of Lynne's wedding. Would he dance with her, and bring her a glass of champagne? At the end of the evening, would he take her home to that sleek, sophisticated bedroom, and make love to her, and then tell her there was an acre of emerald satin in her eyes?

'Stop it, Julie,' she ordered herself. 'There's no future in this sort of awkward speculation.'

This invitation puzzled her, she had to admit. She had refused once. Why had Annabel Hastings written her this note?

'Well, you're going to have to do without knowing,' she told herself firmly. 'Because you are *not* going to run the gauntlet of the Hastings clan just for the doubtful pleasure of finding out why Annabel seems to want you there.'

Or, she reminded, for the even more problematic pleasure of seeing Greg.

A car engine purred into the drive, and Dudley romped towards the garden gate, barking hysterically. Once he reassured himself that the thing on the other side of the gate was human, however, he abased himself in the dust on the path in his excited desire to be picked up and fussed over.

Julie followed him to the gate, half afraid of who would be there. Then she pulled Dudley out of the way and beckoned the visitor to come in. 'Do you often make house calls, Dr Myers?' she asked. 'And on Saturday, no less.'

The vet grinned. 'Not regularly,' he admitted. 'But Leicester is a special case.' He stooped over the old dog, stretched out in the sunshine, to inspect the surgical scars, and then picked up the wriggling puppy.

'He's certainly never going to make a watchdog,' Julie said. 'He barks till someone pays attention to him, and then he melts and licks hands. You should warn his new owners.' She paused, and sadness clutched at her heart. 'That's what you've come for, isn't it? To take him to his new home?'

'Not today. Why? Are you anxious to get rid of him?' The doctor sat down on the porch step with the puppy on his knee. 'He's a healthy little specimen.'

'He's a sweetheart. I'm not eager to lose him, no, but I'm afraid if you leave him much longer I'll be too attached to let him go.'

The vet grinned sympathetically. 'They can do that to you, can't they?'

Julie tried to return the smile. 'This one especially.' She stroked the dog's long, soft ear. 'When are they going to want him?'

'Well, that's what I came to talk to you about. They changed their minds, and now they don't want him at all. I don't suppose you would want to keep him, would you?'

It surprised her, the gladness and relief that welled up in her heart. It was the first time she had let herself realise just how much she would miss this tiny animal, and how quickly he had manipulated his way into her life. 'Yeah,' she said, 'I'll keep him.'

The vet grinned. 'I thought you might,' he drawled. 'Shall we have a formal christening? I never have understood his name.'

'Haven't you? The Earl of Leicester's family name was Dudley.'

The puppy started to gently worry her finger, as if

it was a succulent steak bone. 'You didn't happen to plan this, did you?' Julie asked suspiciously. 'Are you willing to swear that there really was a family who agreed to take him? Cross your heart and all?'

'Well—' the vet said. 'Tell you what, Julie, stop over at the clinic some day next week and ask the receptionist for his registration papers.'

'Papers? He's pure bred? You told me that he was abandoned on the clinic doorstep!'

'No, I didn't,' he said defensively. 'I told you that his owner dropped him off, and that was precisely true.'

'What kind of idiot pays kennel and registration fees and then gives the dog away?'

'One who knows you better than I do,' the vet said promptly. 'He was sure that you'd never willingly adopt another dog, but if you once took a pup home you wouldn't want to let go of him. I would never have thought of it.'

'He— who?' Julie said. This was beginning to sound suspicious, and she didn't think she was going to like the answer.

'I promised I wouldn't say.'

She glared at him. 'As if there was any doubt. I ought to dump this animal on Greg Roberts' doorstep!'

'I thought it was an ingenious idea.' The man sounded quite pleased with himself.

'I have it on the best authority that Greg has always wanted a dog,' she went on bitterly.

Dudley looked up at her with big, sad eyes and laid a paw on her arm. Julie melted. 'All right,' she said. 'It isn't your fault that you were paid for and used by a scheming, conniving—' She saw the interest in Dr Myers' eyes and stopped abruptly.

'I thought Roberts was a nice sort,' he offered helpfully. 'It was very considerate of him to go to all the trouble, I thought. If you hadn't wanted the dog, he'd have been out a bundle of money.'

'He can afford it.'

'I had the impression that night at the clinic that you thought he was pretty special, too,' the doctor went on. 'Well, I'd better be off. Don't be too hard on the man. I think it takes a pretty generous person to go to all this trouble. But to do something like this and keep it secret—that's really unusual.'

'Don't worry,' she said. 'You didn't break your promise. I won't breathe a word to him.'

I won't have the chance, she thought.

She sat there for a long time in the late afternoon sun. Dudley went to sleep in her lap, worn out with the exercise and fresh air.

A pretty generous person, the vet had said. *To do something like this and keep it secret...*

He did it because he knew how important it was to me to have another dog, she thought. He had known it more surely than she herself had. And, because he cared about the things that were important to her, he had gone to a great deal of trouble to arrange the gift in a way she would accept.

Oh, stop it, she told herself. You're going to make yourself crazy this way.

She shut the puppy in the kitchen and went upstairs, still arguing with herself. It wasn't as if she would be crashing the party, one side of her brain argued. She had been invited. But she was going for the wrong reasons, her conscience reminded. She really didn't care if Annabel had a nice birthday. She only wanted to look at Greg a little, and to see if she could observe something different about him.

A new softness in his eyes, no doubt, she mocked herself, which would send her into his arms for ever. It sounded like a scene from a bad movie, complete with swelling music and slow motion!

At least I'll know, she told herself. When I see him again, and there isn't any change, I'll know that I did the right thing. Then I can stop driving myself insane with this wondering.

That's nuts, the other half of her brain said. Go to Annabel Hastings' home, with the whole family watching, in the hope of being able to study Greg Roberts as if he was a microbe on a laboratory slide? Take two aspirin and go to bed, and you'll be over this mad compulsion by morning.

She didn't, of course. She stripped her shorts and shirt off, stepped into the shower, and poured a capful of shampoo over her hair. She worked it into a glorious pile of suds, letting handfuls of bubbles slide down over her shoulders in a luxurious cascade. She was humming in sort of a tuneless little murmur, in time with the pulsing of the water, and when the water sputtered and stopped flowing altogether, she was so absorbed in her thoughts that it took her an instant to realise it.

In the sudden, cold silence, she turned round and stared at the shower head, where a few random drops clung tenaciously and then fell, one by one, into the puddle of shampoo suds that had gathered round her toes.

'Oh, come on,' she said impatiently and twisted the shower controls round the full circle. There was a spatter of water droplets, and then the hissing groan of air in the plumbing pipes.

She stood there feeling foolish for a full minute before she realised that her careless manipulation of the faucets meant that if the water came back on abruptly she could scald herself. She turned the shower off completely and with her fingertips scraped as much of the mountain of suds out of her hair as she could. There was still enough soap to sculpt her hair into the most elaborate headdress ever dreamed of, without benefit of pins or combs. Now what was she to do? she wondered.

'All right,' she said out loud, 'if this is supposed to be a message telling me that I shouldn't go to this party, I can take a hint. I won't go. Now, can I finish my shower?'

The pipes, predictably, stayed silent. She swore and climbed out. The bathroom sink yielded a single noisy spurt and then only the rumble of air.

Julie wiped off as much soap as she could with a damp washcloth, wrapped herself in a terry robe, and went downstairs to call the waterworks' emergency number to find out what had happened. The line was busy. She realised that she was thirsty, and groaned at her own suggestibility. 'I drink tea, I drink coffee, I drink ginger ale,' she moaned, 'and the minute the water stops, none of those things will do. I want a tall glass of cold water!'

She snapped her fingers. Randie always kept a pitcher of water in the refrigerator. Privately, Julie thought it was a nuisance, and she swore under her breath every time she had to move it around the refrigerator to make room. 'I'll never say anything nasty about Randie's habits again,' she pledged, 'if she only remembered to refill the pitcher this time.'

It was full to the brim. Julie stuck a finger in it and winced at the thought of the cold liquid pouring over her sensitive scalp. But her head was already starting to itch from the drying shampoo; she didn't want to wait for the water to warm.

She stooped over the sink and raised the pitcher. The first gush of icy water brought tears to her eyes and a seldom-used word to her lips. A moment later, the bell beside the back door rang.

There is no law, she told herself, that requires me to answer the door. She raised the pitcher again, closed her eyes, and sloshed cold water over her head.

Within thirty seconds a fist started to pound on the glass, and a voice came faintly through the door. 'Dammit, Julie, answer the door. I'm trying to do you a favour!'

She pushed her hair out of her eyes and looked over her shoulder. She realised Greg could see her. She could see him, too, and he looked furious. She pulled the door open. 'This had better be important,' she said.

'You might want to stockpile some water,' he said. 'There's a broken water main up the street, and—' He stopped and took in the scene, from her hair, which dripped sudsy water, to her toes, which were coated with drying soap. 'I see you already know it,' he added weakly.

'Congratulations. You couldn't have arranged it at a more inconvenient time.'

'Wait a minute. You don't think I planned this, do you?'

'I wouldn't be surprised. If you'll excuse me, I was rinsing my hair.' She picked up the pitcher again.

He leaned against the refrigerator door. 'Why do you always assume these things are my fault?'

'Because nine times out of ten, they are. Tell the truth—your construction guys did it just to get even with me, right?' She tipped the pitcher and howled at the sensation in her scalp.

'It certainly wasn't on purpose. But it did happen up at the construction site, yes.'

'And it's Saturday,' she mourned. 'I thought we were safe from your bag of tricks on the weekends.'

'We're pushing to get the building topped off.'

'I suppose I should be grateful the crew has finished next door.'

'They haven't, actually. But they're almost done.'

'What's next?'

'That depends.'

'On whether I sell you the house, right?' She sighed. Why had she even let herself think that his attitude might have changed? 'Look, I'm trying to wash the shampoo out of my hair, so if you'd just go away—'

'I've got a better solution to the problem, if you're interested.'

'I don't feel like driving out to Gray's Lake for a dip this afternoon, but thanks, anyway.'

'I have a perfectly good shower in my apartment.'

She looked up with exasperation in her eyes. 'Do you mean you still have water? This is patently unfair! They could at least have knocked out the whole city while they were at it.'

'You can use all you want,' he said. 'It's going to be hours before the main is fixed.'

'Terrific,' she said glumly.

'Since it was my fault, in a way, that you're out of water, and since you're obviously getting ready to go somewhere, it's the least I can do.'

'I am not getting ready to go somewhere. I was, but I've changed my mind.' There's certainly no need to go to Annabel's party, she was thinking. I've seen more than enough of him, right in my own kitchen, to last me a year.

There was a long silence, and then he said, huskily, 'If I'd known this was going to happen, I'd have arranged a come-as-you-are party. Do you know how delectable you look in that soap? As if you'd been dressed in whipped cream, that's how—'

Her insides started to quiver. It's not fair, she thought, that he can do this to me. All he has to do is look at me and I melt like a hot fudge sundae at a picnic… I shouldn't even think about going to his apartment.

'I'd hate for you to miss your date,' he said.

Part of her wanted to tell him that it wasn't a date at all, that it was him she had wanted to see. But she had too much pride for that. It didn't seem to bother him that she was going out; very well, she would hold her head up and not let him see how his careless comments had affected her.

'Thanks, anyway,' she said. 'But I can't just go walking into your apartment building like this.'

'That's easy enough. Wrap your hair in a towel, and everyone will think you're just coming up from the pool.' He stooped over Dudley's bed and scratched the puppy's ears. 'How are you doing, old pal?' he asked. The puppy whimpered and licked his hand.

'He remembers you,' Julie said icily. Greg looked innocent.

Her head was itchy. What did it matter? she told herself. At least she could get rid of the shampoo. She wrapped a bath towel around her head. 'I'll go and get my clothes.'

When she came back with a tote bag, he was scratching Dudley's chin. The puppy looked lazily ecstatic, and his mournful expression had lightened a little.

'He has to go in his pen,' Julie said. 'Randie's gone for the weekend, so when I leave, it's prison for the puppy.'

Dudley protested loudly, but was stowed safely in the pen. He was sitting in the corner of it, looking after them with sad and quiet dignity, when they left.

'I'll take my car and meet you in the parking ramp,' she offered.

Greg shook his head. 'Too much trouble. I'll run you back home when you're done.'

She shrugged and got into his car. She wasn't fool enough to stand in her driveway in her bathrobe and argue about it, and she'd much rather not have to explain her lack of attire to a traffic officer, either.

'Where's Randie?' he asked as he negotiated the traffic.

He probably didn't care, Julie thought, but it made a little friendly conversation, and that was much better than silence. 'Staying with friends.'

'When is she coming home?'

'Why? Do you want to make another stab at getting her half of the house?'

'Perhaps.'

'I really don't know when she'll be back. She hasn't been talking to me much.' She stared out of the window. 'You've been arguing about the house.'

'That wasn't what I said. She just hasn't made definite plans.'

Sneaking into Greg's apartment in a bathrobe wasn't as difficult as Julie had expected. No one even raised an eyebrow, which should have made her feel relieved. Instead, she was piqued. Just how many women come and go here, anyway? she wondered, with a whisper of jealousy. Was it such a large number that no one bothered to notice any more?

She averted her eyes from the kidney-shaped tub in the centre of the bathroom, unwilling to think about what had happened the last time she had been here. The water in the shower was hot, and the spray was needle-sharp. She stood under it until she couldn't stay a second longer.

I shouldn't have come, she thought. I don't want to face him again. I would have been better off with the memories…

She had locked the bathroom door. Stupid, she thought as she towelled herself dry with unnecessary force. As if he would try to open that door. He doesn't care. You were only a means to an end, and now that you've made it clear that seduction did him no good, he won't waste his time any more.

It was less painful to tell herself that than to think about the possibility that he loved her, too. He couldn't, she told herself crisply. If he did, he wouldn't let this obstacle keep us apart.

The sleek bedroom was quiet, and on the bed her clothes were neatly spread, just as she had left them.

No, not quite as she had left them. On top of her red sundress was a wooden box that she had never seen before, an intricately carved rectangular chest about six inches wide and half as long again.

She picked it up gingerly, as if she expected it to explode in her hands. It was heavy, and the lid opened silently under her fingers.

It was divided in half, and it was lined with emerald green velvet. In the left compartment lay an intricately cut crystal paperweight, its deep facets catching the sunlight and slicing it into rainbows. On the other side was a crystal pendant in the shape of a teardrop, surrounded by a delicate gold framework and supported by a gleaming chain. Each deeply cut crevice in the crystal was inlaid with a tiny gold wire, giving depth and colour to the necklace. Tiny diamonds were scattered over the framework and nestled in the crevices.

It's beautiful, she thought. And it's the strangest combination I've ever seen. A paperweight and a necklace, together?

In the lid of the box, in tiny, engraved letters on a gold plate, were the words, *'Out of destruction, sometimes beauty comes'*.

The vase, she thought. He had taken the worthless, broken pieces of that Bavarian crystal vase, and he had created this thing of beauty.

Her hands were trembling so much that she had to set the box down. Tears blurred her eyes and then overflowed. He *does* understand, she thought. He's not a stubborn, selfish brute—or at least, he's been no more stubborn than I have. I wasn't willing to even try to look at things from his point of view.

I can hang on to my house, she thought, and give up the other things—a man to love, a child to nurse, a home to share. Without family, it will never be more than a house. Or I can let it go, and embark on a new adventure, with a man I love. I can keep the lonely memories, or I can let go of them, and live. If I only have Greg, I can make a home wherever he is—here in this apartment, or somewhere else. It isn't the four walls that are important, it is the people within. And if I don't have Greg, then there isn't much of anything left.

She took the pendant from the box and fastened the chain carefully around her throat. Perhaps he'll know, she thought as she dressed, what it means for me to have put it on. I'm not sure I can explain it, but I'll have to try.

He was waiting in the living-room for her, staring out across the city to where the lowering sun peeped through the indolent clouds, turning them into bits of hammered gold.

When she came in, he turned quickly, and the tension seemed to melt out of him when he saw the pendant gleaming at her throat. 'I love you, Julie,' he whispered. 'I want to spend my life with you.'

She came across to him, determined to quickly tell him what she had to say. 'You're right,' she said. 'Sometimes progress isn't a bad thing. You can—have the house, Greg—' There had been a momentary hesitation; she couldn't bear to frame the words, *you can tear it down.* 'I love you, too.' Her throat was too choked to speak, and then there was no need. His arms were round her, and she was safe in that haven that had given her such comfort.

'My God, how I've missed you,' he said, when at last their first hungry kiss was at an end.

Julie could hardly breathe, much less speak.

'My grandmother,' he mused, 'is a very wise woman.'

'I can't figure her out,' Julie said huskily. 'She stopped you from leaving with me that day. And yet she wanted me to come to her party tonight.'

'Damn the party,' he said. 'I want to stay here and make love to you.' He brushed her tangled curls back with fingers that were almost trembling. 'She didn't want me to go with you that day, because she was afraid I would carelessly mess up something I should be taking very seriously,' he said. 'She didn't know that, when I walked in that afternoon and saw you there talking to her, I realised for the first time that you were no casual fling. I knew I needed you in my life always.'

'You, too?' she whispered. 'That was the day—'

'''Simple problems have simple solutions'',' he quoted, and laughed.

It struck a sad chord in her, and she bit her lip. A very simple solution, she thought, with a trace of bitterness. Julie gives in, and all is well. She tried to ignore the feeling, and pulled him closer, in the hope that this awful doubt would go away.

He kissed her quickly. 'They'll start work Monday,' he said. 'I'll show you what I have in mind, and I'm sure you'll have some ideas, too.'

Julie was horrified. 'Greg, I—it's going to take some time! I can't just snap my fingers and be moved out. I've got the shop to worry about, and then there's Randie. We'll have to find a place for Randie—'

'Randie is welcome to live with us as long as she likes.'

'That's wonderful, but it isn't a solution.'

He put a finger across her lips to still her protests. 'You're not moving, Julie. You're not going anywhere.'

He was smiling, but it took her a minute to comprehend it. 'I'm not?'

'No. It was a beautiful gesture, offering to let me tear the house down because you want me even more than you want it. But how long do you think you'd have been contented with that decision?'

She gulped, and admitted shakily, 'About five minutes.'

'Was it that long? I thought I saw you wavering before then.' He pinched her cheek gently. 'That's part of what I love about you, anyway—your determination to keep the past alive. Grandmother pointed that out to me the afternoon we had our last fight. She let me rage for a while about how stubborn and unreasonable you were being, and then she reminded me that I wasn't being exactly rational myself, in trying to have both you and the office building. She made it plain to me that I had to choose. I've chosen.'

He paused for an instant, and then confessed unsteadily, 'But there really wasn't any choice to make, Julie. Building things has always been important to me. But without you—' He shook his head, and said, more softly, 'Without you, there just doesn't seem to be any point to living at all.'

She pressed her hands against her face, trying to believe that it wasn't just another dream. 'So what are you going to do?' she asked breathlessly.

'We are going to expand the garden over the whole area where the car park was,' he said. 'Just as it used to be.'

He had remembered her telling him that. A tiny flicker of happiness came to life inside her, and began to grow.

'On the other side, we are going to build a garage, so your car doesn't have to make a trip into storage every year. If you'd like, we can add a new shop for you, so we won't be tripping over customers any more. Then we'll—'

'We're really going to live there?' She felt as if there was a giant bubble of happiness expanding inside her chest and threatening to choke her.

'Yes, my love. Unless you have other ideas?' Greg was tentative, diffident, and the sudden humility in his voice convinced her of his sincerity more surely than any number of elaborate plans could have. It's true, her heart was singing. It's really true that he loves me, as much as I love him—enough to give up something important because I hate it, even though he doesn't quite understand.

She traced the frown lines in his forehead with a gentle fingertip, and smiled up at him, and he pulled her even closer, as if to say that she would never escape from him again.

'But don't you mind?' she whispered, with one last twinge of doubt. 'All the money you've put into this project—'

'Don't remind me. I've already fired the estate agent who kept telling me he had the whole thing under control and I'd have clear title any day now, so I should go ahead with the construction plans.'

It puzzled her. 'But I never—'

'Including your house. It seems he'd talked to you once, and you'd told him to go jump in the lake—'

She remembered, then. 'It was the Raccoon River, actually,' she murmured. 'And I told him to drown himself.'

'But he didn't tell me that. Instead, he told me you were holding out for more money, but that he was certain you'd come around when the price was right.'

She released a long breath. 'So that's why you were so sure that I was playing games.'

'That's right. And I was furious when you kept stalling and holding up my work. If I'd had any idea you'd told him the house was not for sale, I'd never have started the project at all. I am neither a blockhead nor a robber baron.'

'But then we wouldn't have got to know each other,' she said.

He kissed her, hard. 'Don't bet on it. But that's also why I was confused when I met a gorgeous, sexy lady named Julie at my cousin's wedding, and then found out that she was really the hard-nosed Juliet Gordon who was holding up my new project.'

'You didn't know? I was sure Lynne had arranged it.'

'I'm sure she did, but it had nothing to do with the house. Not that she had to arrange anything; I'd already spotted you. In any case, she didn't have a chance to tell me your name.'

'You got so quiet that night,' she remembered. 'I thought it was because Keith was finally gone and you could stop playing a part.'

'No,' he said. 'It was because I was afraid I'd been conned. I'm pretty well known in this town, Julie, and when I found out that you had every reason in the world to want to strike up an acquaintance with me—You had said you wanted money and influence and power. My instincts said you were lying, but when I found out who you were...'

She sighed, and relaxed against him. He rubbed his cheek against her hair. 'It still didn't make any difference,' he confessed softly. 'I think I'd fallen half in love with you already. The next day I came out to the house, determined to bargain, and then there was no turning back, though I didn't quite realise it then.'

'I wanted so badly for you to believe that Keith didn't matter.'

'I knew you couldn't really love him. I was just afraid you might not know that.'

'And you really don't mind if we keep the house?'

He shrugged. 'It has probably cost me less this way than it would to build a new one somewhere else. I'll still buy Randie's half, of course.'

'That's sweet of you,' she murmured. 'She wants that apartment so badly.'

'Sweet, nothing. I'm protecting myself in case you get mad at me and want to throw me out! And I've already got the plans in the works for an office tower on the other side of the one we're building now.' He felt her stiffen in his arms, and added, 'There are no houses there now—they were torn down thirty years ago.'

'That's all right, then.' She bit her lip. 'You sound as if you've thought it out very carefully,' she said doubtfully. 'But how do I know you mean it? What if you resent me later because you're stuck with this house, as I would have resented you if I'd given it up? I'm afraid, Greg.'

He traced her profile with a gentle fingertip, and said, suddenly very serious, 'Don't be. I've never had a chance to get attached to a place the way you have. I'm sort of looking forward to putting down some real roots.'

For a moment, he was the little boy whose mother had stifled him and whose father had no time for him. Julie wanted to cry. 'I love you,' she whispered.

He gave her a lecherous grin, and the little boy was gone. 'We'll have to have a house some day,' he pointed out, and pulled her down into the nest of floor cushions. 'We're just planning ahead. We can't raise kids in a condo.'

'We can't?' she said shyly. She could hardly speak for the memories of what it had been like the last time they had lain together in those cushions, with the breakfast tray pushed carelessly aside.

'No. They couldn't even have a dog, for crying out loud. And if you think I'm going to find another home for Robert Dudley, First Earl of Leicester, after all the trouble I had giving him to you, you're crazy.'

'You've been talking to Dr Myers.'

'Nope. I've been doing my research. Was he named for me, just a little bit?' he asked hopefully. 'The Robert part?'

She thought, a little hazily, that she was probably giving off a glow of happiness so bright that it was lighting up the side of the building. 'I'll never tell.'

He growled playfully against her throat, and then pulled her up out of the cushions. 'Much as I would like to spend the evening right here making love to you,' he said, 'I think we owe it to my grandmother to tell her that we're finally on the right track. She told me again this afternoon that I should marry you, you know. She said it would help me settle down.'

'She did? And what did you think of that?' She pulled her skirt down straight.

He was watching her with a warm gleam in his eyes. 'I think it will be a definitely unsettling experience. Nevertheless, will you marry me anyway, Juliet? Love, honour, and obey, and all that stuff?'

'Not obey,' she warned.

'Well,' he said cheerfully, 'I thought it was worth

a try. Would you at least promise not to go to law school? I don't mind if you picket me now and then, but if you were to drag me into court over every new project, I don't think I could handle it.' He opened the apartment door with a grand gesture. 'After you, my love.'

'If you don't want me to be mad at you, don't threaten to tear down historical things.'

'If that's all it takes to keep you happy,' he murmured, 'this will be a marriage made in heaven.'

'That,' she said, 'and a little of your time now and then.'

He saw the look in her eyes, and kicked the door shut, turning to take her into his arms. 'The heck with it,' he said. 'We're going to be late to the party.'

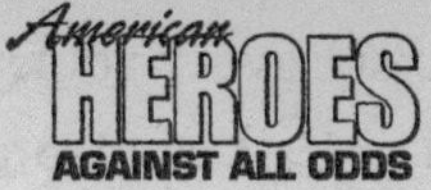
American
HEROES
AGAINST ALL ODDS